CLARK SELBY

BOOK FIVE

DANGEROUS MISSION

Dangerous Mission
Copyright © 2024 by Clark Selby

Library of Congress Control Number: 2024923639

ISBN
978-1-964982-92-2 (Paperback)
978-1-964982-93-9 (eBook)
978-1-964982-91-5 (Hardcover)

Dedication

This Book is dedicated to the men and women, who Serve to Protect our Freedom, the CIA, FBI, U.S. Military and Police Officers, and for my wife, Karen Serene Selby who helps with all of my books.

TABLE OF CONTENTS

Chapter 1...1
Chapter 2...8
Chapter 3.. 14
Chapter 4...29
Chapter 5...37
Chapter 6...45
Chapter 7...53
Chapter 8...63
Chapter 9...71
Chapter 10...76
Chapter 11...81
Chapter 12...86
Chapter 13...90
Chapter 14...97
Chapter 15... 102
Chapter 16... 106
Chapter 17... 111
Chapter 18... 115
Chapter 19... 120
Chapter 20... 124
Chapter 21... 128
Chapter 22... 134
Chapter 23... 137
Chapter 24... 142
Chapter 25... 149
Chapter 26... 153

1

T
om Parker was at last enjoying his life and why not, he earned the privilege after spending a lifetime of service for his country. Twenty years in the army and untold number of years working for the CIA.

Tom's father was a three star General in the army, who was awarded the Medal of Honor for his action in Korea, which gave Tom the opportunity to attend West Point.

There, he graduated in the middle of his class. In Vietnam, Tom was a captain and serving as an aide to General Westmoreland, a longtime friend of Tom's father.

General Westmoreland, gave him a battlefield promotion to Lieutenant Colonel to serve as the commander of the Special Forces in Vietnam.

Tom wasn't eligible to become a major yet, but Westmoreland could do whatever he wanted because he was *the man* in Vietnam.

Tom saw lots of action in Vietnam, had been put into areas that became some of the worse battles in the war there.

He saved several of the men serving under him and was awarded every medal a combat soldier could get, everything except the Medal of Honor.

He was left to fight his way out of one battle after another, one battle he had successfully evacuated all his wounded men out of the battleground on helicopters.

The other men under his command were able to join troops coming in as reinforcement as Tom stayed with the ones who had been cut off and wounded.

As he later told his wounded men after he made it safely back, it was a long walk back by himself.

During the Gulf War, as he was finishing his twenty years in the army and working with the CIA, he was asked to join the CIA.

They told him when he joined the CIA, once you've joined, the only way out is to die. They could call on him at any minute and any time. He found out all about it a couple of years ago; just how lucky he was to still be alive. It was a miracle after all the times he had been in harm's way.

Lucky, yeah, Tom was really lucky! He was married to Jenny, a beautiful Hong Kong billionaire and they had a great looking three-year-old son.

They lived most of the time in their mansion in Beverly Hills and other times in Jenny's Hong Kong penthouse, when her company needed her there.

What a far cry from the places he had lived in the past.

Jenny's first husband died in a car crash in Vietnam after finishing a deal to build several new companies there. Jenny's father and father-in-law stepped in to help Jenny run her husband's company and were able to help provide the money for her to become the largest landowner in the Orient.

Jenny's company held properties in Hong Kong and owned property in all of the major cities in China, Vietnam, Singapore and Korea, as well as building and operating a casino with the North Korean's Government, located on a small island off the coast of North Korea and China.

Jenny was one of the richest women in the world and her company continued to grow and become more profitable every year.

Jenny met Tom while he was working in Hong Kong trying to stop dangerous cargo from being shipped into the USA by al-Qeada. In addition to helping run her companies, she was acting as the Security Director for the Port of Hong Kong.

After meeting Tom, she offered to help him with his problem and soon fell in love with him and they married.

She had vowed never to get married again and was raising her daughter alone, but love finds a way even if you never plan to fall in love again.

Coming to Los Angeles with Tom and her daughter, Jackie, she found she liked America and Beverly Hills so she bought a huge mansion and they lived there.

Her daughter Jackie really liked living and shopping in Beverly Hills and earned a law degree from Harvard.

Like her daughter, Jenny was an attorney so she was a woman who almost always got her own way.

Jenny kept her penthouse in one of her Hong Kong buildings and they would travel there whenever she needed to attend to business that required her presence.

Traveling wasn't a problem. Jenny or Tom, just called their pilots to get the Gulfstream V ready and they were off to any place in the world an hour later.

Yes sir, Tom was beyond being lucky, he was blessed!

Tom's step-daughter, Jackie, had finished law school at Harvard and was now practicing law with a Beverly Hills law firm who worked with the stars.

Jackie lived with them, so except for Tom's parents, all of his loved ones were together with him.

They tried to get Tom's parents to move to California, but they didn't want to be away from their long-time friends in Maryland.

Besides, as his dad said, he probably wouldn't be able to find any new friends in California that he could beat at golf.

Dad loved his golf and mom loved her friends. So they would stay in Maryland.

On a glorious sunny California morning, Tom was relaxing by the pool reading his morning paper waiting for Jenny and Tom, Jr. to have breakfast.

Robert Fong appeared with a telephone in his hand.

"Mister Tom, there's a call for you from a Mister Ron Parsons." Robert handed the phone to Tom.

"Hello Ron, it's been a long time since we last spoke, so what kind of a problem do you and the company have now?

"Tom!" I'm surprised you'd think the only time I'd call was when we had a problem at the CIA."

"I've known you for too many years, Ron Parsons. You never have time for idle chit chat."

"All right, Tom, you know me too well. Yes, we've got a problem and I need your help."

"OK, what's screwed up or who's screwing it up?"

"Now Tom, you know we never do that. Sometimes we just have to go in a little different direction and sometimes I have to have a different agent to change the direction. So I thought of you."

"Ron, if you thought of me, it must really be screwed up."

"OK, it is really screwed up, and it will be a really dangerous mission for you to try to fix."

"What's your problem?"

"Tom, it's not just my problem, it's a problem for the President of the United States. In the past we've been helping a cleric by the name of al-Garde to build an army to help us in Afghanistan. Now he has turned on us, and he thinks we don't know it.

"He is still playing footsy with our local CIA Agent, Harold La Blanc. He's got Harold believing he is still on our side. We lost seven soldiers last week in a firefight with some of al-Garde's men."

"So, why does Agent La Blanc think he's still on our side?"

"Because Harold is the one who recruited al-Garde and he's too close to see what's happening. Al-Garde told Harold it was an accident his men attacked and killed the patrol.

"It wasn't an accident. We have a man in al-Garde's camp who reports to another one of our agents, Mike Jones, on what's going on with al-Garde's rank and file soldiers.

"Al-Garde personally gave the orders to attack and kill all of the members of the patrol because he thought we were getting too close to some high-ranking al-Qaeda officers."

"OK, Ron so what do you want me to do?"

"I'll tell you what I want you to do, get our ass out of this mess we're in without it looking like the company or America had anything to do with killing al-Garde.

"It's got to be blamed on al-Qaeda, so we can keep the army al-Garde built on our side. He's got a good second in command, al-Mazano, we could work with him if we can get rid of al-Garde without him having any idea that we caused al-Garde's death."

"Well Ron, this doesn't sound like the kind of job for an old retired agent like me."

"Yeah, I know, you've got a soft life living with a billionaire wife in Beverly Hills, lying around the pool all day, playing with your son, but you're the luckiest guy the company's ever had.

"You got to do this for me; your country needs you, and, hell, your president needs you! He's the one who gave us al-Garde in the first place. The guy's name came from one of the president's closest friends.

"Al-Garde has to die a blooming hero, so you've got to be sure, he one of our dead heroes, not one of al-Qaeda."

"Ron, I don't think I'm up to this job and God only knows what Jenny will think. This doesn't sound like a walk in the park kind of job to me.

"I'm too damned old for this kind of duty. I know you've got a lot of young tough agents with the company now, so why don't you give the job to one of them?"

"I've got two very good reasons. I'm not giving this job to one of them. First, we don't want any records of this job showing up on the company books; it could look bad to show we killed one of our allies in this battle with al-Qaeda.

"Second, the President asked for you, because he thinks you walk on water or something like that, and if anybody could get it done right, it would be you."

"Just what would make him think something like that?"

"Probably, he got the idea from me. After I told him about how you helped to get Jack Hayes back from al- Qaeda and helped to kill off the

Pakistani Minister of Defense, who was a traitor to his country, and you made America look like a hero at the same time."

"Gee, thanks Ron. You know neither one of these are true, don't you?"

"Well, actually they are true; you were the one in charge of the mission and both of these things happened on your watch.

"So the President trusts you to do this job for him and I trust you can do the job, no matter how dangerous the mission is."

"OK, Ron, I'll talk to Jenny about doing this for you and the President, but you're really a coward or you would talk to Jenny for me."

"I know, Tom, but that's why you're a hero and I am sitting at a desk in Langley, Virginia and sending out hero types like you to do the dirty work when it has to be done."

As Tom was signing off the phone, Jenny and Tom Jr., sat down next to him.

Jenny asked, "What did Ron Parsons want with you? Robert told me you were talking to him."

"He sure didn't just call to say hello, he wants me to go to Afghanistan and kill a cleric. The company recruited him to organize an army, who has now turned to the other side."

"I know you told him 'no', didn't you, Tom? Didn't you?" "Not exactly, I told him I would talk with you about it." "OK, you talked to me. You can't think about leaving me and Tommy here to worry about you. Remember how

close we came to getting killed the last time we went to Afghanistan to find Jack Hayes and you know how much al-Qaeda wants to kill you for killing so many of their top people.

"You know they have a price on your head; it's probably dangerous for you right here in America, as bad as they want to kill you, and going to Afghanistan is just plain stupid!"

"I told Ron you wouldn't be happy if I agreed to go do this for them."

"Thomas Paul Parker! Not happy! That's got to be one of the most understated thing you've said in your entire life."

"It's simple, Jenny. I'll just tell him I'm not going."

"Why would he ask you to do this when they have plenty of agents in the CIA?"

"I guess the President asked for me."

"You mean the President of the United States?"

"That's the one."

"Why would the President ask for you to do this kind of job?"

"Jenny, apparently this cleric was recruited by the company to build an army to help fight al-Qaeda, but somehow he switched sides. Since one of the president's closest friends recommended the cleric, they want me to kill him and make it look like al-Qaeda did it. This way the cleric can be one of our dead heroes and we keep the army he built on our side."

"Sounds like a really dangerous job to me."

"It sounds impossible to me!"

"I guess if anyone could do it, it would be my husband.

What am I saying! I don't want you to go."

"Jenny, it's something I've got to do. We could lose a lot of good soldiers if al-Garda isn't stopped and we could lose his army, which we need to help fight al-Qaeda, if we don't do the job right."

"OK, Tom, I'll go with you as far as Hong Kong, so I can see my folks and Tommy can stay with them while I go with you to Afghanistan."

"Jenny, you know you can't go with me to Afghanistan, it's too dangerous. One of us has to be around to raise Tommy.

"Just watch me!"

Tom said nothing else. He knew no one could stop Jenny when her mind was made up, so he told her to get her things ready, they would be leaving in a couple of hours.

Jenny just smiled.

2

Two hours later Jenny, Tommy and Tom were on the plane headed for Hong Kong to drop Tommy off with Jenny's parents. Tom thought it was wrong letting Jenny go with him to Afghanistan, but he knew she would never agree to let him go without her.

If he heard Jenny say she never wanted to be a widow again ten times, he'd heard her say it a hundred times.

She said if Tom was going to get killed working for the CIA, she wanted to die with him.

Tommy was busy looking out the window trying to see something below them, but there was nothing to see except ocean and the clouds they were flying over.

Tommy was a very good traveler, since he had made the trips from California to Hong Kong many times before.

He had his favorite toys with him and since they were flying straight and level, he could get down on the floor and play all he wanted to.

Jenny was busy as usual, talking on the phone to one of her employees in her Hong Kong office about some project they were starting in Hanoi.

Tom didn't know how she kept up with all of the projects her company had going on throughout the Far East.

He only knew he was glad he didn't have to try keeping up with them all.

Right now, Tom had his own problems: trying to see that someone was killed without making it look like the company had anything to do with it.

Another small problem! How could he make it look like al-Qaeda killed al-Garda, when he was sent by the President of The United States to kill him to get rid of this threat to their operations in Afghanistan?

Wow, what a problem this could be even for Tom Parker, the master of finding ways of getting rid of enemies of America.

Tom thought, right now I probably should be enjoying the time I have with Tommy.

He sure loved being a father, even if it was really late in his life to become a father. He loved that boy with all his heart.

Suddenly, the Gulfstream begin shaking and losing altitude. Tom thought, what the hell is going on as he reached for Tommy, who was crying and rolling on the floor toward the front of the plane.

Jenny reached for Tommy at the same time as Tom did and then their heads collided and knocked her out of her seat and onto the floor.

Tom quickly fastened Tommy into a seat with his seat belt. At the same time he reached down and grabbed Jenny with his left arm and pulled her up from the floor.

Tom was having a hard time picking Jenny up due to the plane diving straight down toward the ocean below them.

Tom stood up and placed Jenny in a seat across from where he and Tommy were sitting.

Tom quickly got back into own his seat and yelled at Jenny to fasten her seat belt and put her head down and hold on to her legs.

At the same time Tom reached Tommy and put his head down on a pillow and told him to hang onto his hand.

Tom yelled back to their flight attendants, Julia Meyers and Crystal Swan, and they both said they were in their seats and buckled up.

Suddenly, the Gulfstream's nose begin coming up from its nose dive and the plane began to level off and flying again in a straight line.

Captain Dean's voice came over the cabin speakers and said, "I'm sorry, folks, but we lost both engines causing us to fall out of the sky like that.

"It took everything we could do to get them restarted. I can add that we're still having trouble with the engines, so we're going to find someplace to get this plane down as soon as we can.

Captain Dean continued, "We're going to keep at this very low altitude, only about four thousand feet above the ocean, just in case both engines stall out again. This way we have a chance of putting the plane down on the ocean without going down nose first."

Tom asked Jenny to come and sit with Tommy while he went up to the cockpit to talk to Captain Dean.

Jenny unfastened her seat belt and moved over next to Tommy, who was sitting very quietly. Not crying or talking, just sitting, not moving or making a sound.

Tom thought he's probably just scared.

Why not, the situation would scare anyone to death.

Tom made his way up to the cockpit and opened the door. He could see both, Captain Roger Dean and CoPilot, Tim Turpin working hard checking everything about their engines they could using their instruments.

Tom asked, "What's going on with the engines, Roger?"

"I sure wish I knew what's happening. Tom, we don't have any idea what's going on with them!"

Tom asked again, "You don't have any idea of what's happening to them?"

"No sir, we were cruising along with everything working great and they just quit and then we started falling out of the sky. Believe me, it took everything Tim and I could do to get them started again and they're still not running the way they should. I'm afraid they're not going to get us to Hong Kong,

"Tom, I'm looking for someplace to put us down as soon as we can without putting us into the drink."

Tom said, "Where are we?"

"I'm working on it right now."

"Roger, have you been in radio contact with anyone since we lost power?"

"No, we haven't had time."

"Don't you think it's a good idea to let somebody known we've got a problem?"

Roger clicked on his microphone and said, "Anchorage Control, this is Gulfstream HGL001, do you read?"

"Gulfstream HGL001, this is Anchorage Control, read you loud and clear."

"Anchorage Control, we are having engine trouble and are now flying at four thousand feet."

Gulfstream, are you declaring an emergency?" Not yet Anchorage, can you find us on radar?

"No, try squawking 1200."

"Roger, Anchorage. Setting, squawk on 1200."

"Gulfstream, sorry we're not picking you up maybe due to your altitude, you may be too low for us to pick up your squawking."

"Thanks anyway, Anchorage, we'll try to climb up higher if we can; we need to know where we are."

"OK, Gulfstream, give us a call when you have …

The radio went dead!

"What happened, Roger?"

"I don't know what happened, except we just lost radio contact with Anchorage!"

Just then both engines shut down and the plane began losing altitude and was headed straight into the ocean.

Tom scrambled out of the cockpit back to where Jenny and Tommy were sitting. He yelled to them and to Julia and Crystal, "We're going into the ocean. Hang on!

Tom got into his seat and fastened his seat belt just as the plane hit the water.

Roger and Tim managed to land the plane in the ocean as if they were landing a sea plane with the nose of the plane up.

They did have some luck when they landed in the ocean, it was very smooth, with only a few small waves.

Tom sprang into action as soon as the plane hit the water. He made sure everyone in the cabin had their life vest on and he checked to see if Roger and Tim were all right. They were.

Tommy sat quietly in his seat, not crying or making any noise. Jenny checked him to be sure he was all right and he was.

Tommy said, "I'm OK, mommy, can we get out now?"

"Yes Tommy, we'll be getting out of the plane and into a little boat."

"OK mommy, that sounds like fun."

Jenny thought to herself, she didn't think it was going to be fun at all."

Julia and Crystal got two small life rafts out of the cargo hold of the plane and brought them to the wing exits.

At the same time, Roger and Tim got the emergency radio transmitter and turned it on. They needed it to help the search planes find their downed plane.

Tom gathered up coats, blankets, and all of the water and food he could find, along with his gun and ammo to put into one of the rubber life rafts.

Tom put his hostler on his belt and holstered his weapon to be sure he had it with him.

Jenny put Tommy's coat on him and gathered up some of his toys to take with them to give him something to do.

Roger said, "We need to be sure to take the flare gun and every flashing light we can find with us.

"Folks, it's time to get out of this plane and time for us to get away from it before it starts sinking. When it goes down it could take our life rafts with it!"

Tom opened the emergency wing exit and helped Julia and Crystal out of the plane. He pushed the life rafts through the exit and they inflated them.

Tom and Jenny began handing out all of the items to Julia and Crystal that they had gathered up to take with them in the rafts.

As soon as the rafts were loaded with their supplies, Tom had Jenny come out of the exit onto the wing.

Then he handed Tommy to her as he climbed through the exit, with Roger and Tim following close behind him.

All of them inflated their life vest as soon as they were standing on the wing of the plane.

Roger told Tom he should get into the life raft, while Tim held the rope of the raft and then he would help get Jenny, Tommy and Julia in the raft with him.

After the four of them were safely in the first raft, then Roger got in the second life raft, while Tim held the line on the raft, so Crystal could safely get into the raft, then Tim would follow.

Everything went fine until it was time for Tim to get into the raft. Tim threw the rope to Crystal he had been using to hold the raft close to the plane, but the raft began floating away from the plane.

Roger tried to paddle the raft back to the plane, but a big wave came and pushed the raft farther away from the plane.

Worse, the wave pushed water over the wing and into the cabin and for the first time the plane began to show signs of sinking.

Tim had no choice. He jumped into the water and began swimming as fast as he could toward the raft with Roger and Crystal in it.

Roger continued paddling toward the plane making the swim closer for Tim.

Crystal picked up the rope Tim had been using before to hold the raft close to the plane and threw it to him.

Tim grabbed the rope and began pulling himself toward the life raft. At the same time Roger and Crystal took hold of the rope to help pull Tim to the raft.

When Tim got next to the raft, Roger and Crystal were able to pull Tim out of the water and into the raft.

Roger immediately began paddling as hard and as fast as he could to get the raft as far away from their downed plane as he could.

As Roger was getting his raft farther away from the plane, Jenny's beautiful plane was slowly slipping into the ocean, then it was gone.

The only thing any of them could see was their two rafts and their fellow companions sitting all alone in a very large ocean with nothing in sight except water.

No land, no plane, no boats, just them.

3

Tom called out to Roger to start paddling toward them and he would paddle his raft to meet him, so they could tie the two rafts together to make both the rafts more stable.

As soon as the two rafts had been secured together, Roger began checking to be sure their radio beacon was operating to signal their location if and when someone began looking for them.

Tom wondered just how long that might be.

It was too bad Anchorage Control couldn't have picked them up on radar before they went down, so they would have had some idea of where to start looking for them.

Tom and Roger talked about what they could do, if anything, considering they didn't know where they were.

Tom was concerned if they started paddling the rafts it would sap their strength and cause them not to be able to survive as long as if they conserved their energy.

So far, everyone remained calm and Tommy was content to be playing with some of his toy cars on the floor of the raft they had managed to bring with them from the plane.

Tom knew it was important to try to keep everyone calm and to stay focused on staying alive. Not easy to do when you're somewhere in the middle of the Bering Sea and all of them knew no one knew where they were.

Meanwhile, back at Anchorage Control, the Flight Controller continued to try to raise them on the radio to no avail.

After trying to make contact with them on the radio for more than an hour, he checked with Honolulu Control, they told him they had not had any communications with his missing aircraft either.

The Anchorage Control Flight Controller contacted the Los Angeles Flight Control to check on the flight plan for Gulfstream HKL001.

He was told the plane had seven people aboard bound for Hong Kong with Captain Roger Dean in command.

After getting this information the Flight Controller contacted his supervisor and gave him all of the information he had on the missing aircraft.

The supervisor immediately declared the aircraft had apparently crashed into the Bering Sea, somewhere near the Aleutian Islands.

He asked all flights in the vicinity to be alert and listen for a signal from a downed aircraft, then sat back in his chair and said a silent prayer for the safety of the seven souls aboard the plane.

The information was flashed to FFA Headquarters in Washington D.C. regarding the missing plane.

From there the information was sent to several federal agencies, including the CIA Headquarters.

When the ID Number of the plane, HGL-001, came into the CIA Central Computer, the computer sounded an alarm identifying the plane as belonging to CIA Retired Agent Tom Parker wife's company.

The computer operator on duty printed off the information regarding the missing plane and took a copy directly to the Assistant Director of CIA, Ron Parsons.

Ron took one look at the printed message and picked up a phone and called CIA's Communications Center and told the operator on duty to check for Tom Parker's microchip ID number, by using their satellite tracking system to find his location.

Ron remembered they had inserted an agent ID microchip under Tom's skin on his left shoulder a long time ago, because he had been sent on so many dangerous missions and he was always hard to keep track of.

Less than ten minutes passed before the communications center operator called Ron back and gave him the coordinates of Tom's location.

Ron then called the Coast Guard's Headquarters and asked for the air-sea rescue duty officer. Ron explained one of his CIA Operative's private plane crashed off of the southwest coast of the Aleutian Islands, and gave the duty officer the coordinates of Tom's location. He asked if they could please pick Tom and the other six people.

The Coast Guard Duty Officer didn't even ask Ron how he knew where Tom and the others were.

He just sent a flash message to a Coast Guard patrol plane nearest the area where the plane went down.

The pilot changed course and headed directly to the coordinates they were given, and radioed a Coast Guard

cutter operating in the area of their destination, asking them to be ready to pick up seven people from a downed plane.

The Coast Guard cutter was ready to return to port when they received the radio message about the location of a downed plane.

The skipper of the cutter gave the command to turn around and make full speed toward the coordinates given her.

Lt. Commander Sessions began giving orders to get everything ready for an air-sea rescue including their helicopter.

She knew it was getting very dark and only wondered if they could get to the site before it was completely dark.

It was bad enough fishing people out of the water in the daylight and a lot worse in the dark.

In the meantime, Tom and the rest of the folks in the two life rafts were trying to make the best of a bad situation.

All they could do was hope someone would pick up the signal indicating a downed plane.

Tom could see the swells beginning to pick up as night was drawing nearer.

Tom told everyone to take some of the extra rope they brought with them from the plane and tie themselves onto the rope around the rafts before the ocean got any rougher.

He wanted to be sure that if the waves got too rough and anyone was tossed out of a life raft they could be easily retrieved.

Jenny put a rope through Tommy belt and tied it to the rope on the life raft, then did the same for herself.

In a few minutes everyone had been secured with a rope tied to them and to the rafts.

The timing seemed to be perfect as a huge wave came and picked the two rafts straight out of the water and dropped them five or six feet straight back down, flooding water over the rafts and taking everything not tied down with it.

There went all of their food and water, but all the seven passengers were safely still secured in the rafts.

They were all just wet and left to wonder how long they could survive without help now that their food and water were gone.

Tom's luck was holding; he heard a plane in the distance and it seemed to be coming directly toward them.

Everyone started shouting and waving as the plane began circling around them, wagging its wings to let them know they saw them.

The waves continued to build, coming one right after another.

Tom thought we better get some help soon or it's going to be really hard to get us out of the water.

A few seconds later Tom heard another familiar sound, the whirling of a helicopter's blades.

He couldn't see it yet, but he knew that sound meant help would soon be there.

It was a sound anyone who fought in Nam knew well. More than once Tom had been saved by a chopper.

Tom thought it was one of the most beautiful sounds in the world.

The helicopter broke through a big dark cloud and began descending directly toward the two rafts.

Everyone in the rafts except Tom and Tommy began shouting and waving at the people in the helicopter.

Tom simply smiled and sat back against the side of the raft's small side wall.

Tommy sat and watched his mother and acted like he couldn't decide why she was so excited and yelling and waving at a helicopter.

Tommy would soon find out why.

As the helicopter hovered off to one side of the rafts, three people jumped out of the chopper into the ocean below them.

As soon as the three people were in the water, they began swimming toward the rafts.

The first one to arrive was a young woman who asked if there was anyone injured.

"No." was the resounding reply.

"Good," she said.

Then she said, "Let's see if we can get all of you aboard the chopper."

By that time the two other sailors with her had reached the rafts and were holding onto the sides of the rafts.

The woman waved her right arm to the men standing in the open doorway of the helicopter and they started lowering a cable down toward the rafts.

One of the men swam out to where the cable came into the water and swam back to the raft towing the cable with him.

The woman said, "OK, I want one of you three women to put on this harness, so we can get you aboard the chopper."

Crystal and Julia cried out, "Take Jenny first!"

Jenny said, "No, I'll wait until I can take Tommy with me."

The Coast Guard woman said, "Listen, ladies, I don't give a damn about who goes first, you're all going, so one of you get into this damn harness."

"Tom said, "OK, I tell you what, sailor, I'll take Tommy with me first and then these ladies will be happy to follow your orders, OK?"

"I guess that will be just great, if you will kindly start moving your ass so we can all get on the chopper."

Tom quickly put on the harness, hooked it to the cable, took Tommy in his arms and said, "OK, let's go."

The female sailor waved her right arm and then put her right thumb up to signal to the men in the chopper to take up the cable.

The cable began pulling Tom and Tommy up out of the raft and straight up to the helicopter.

Arriving at the helicopter one of the sailors took a long pole with a hook on it and hooked the cable pulling Tom and Tommy through the door of the helicopter.

Then the sailors unhooked the cable from Tom's harness and sent the cable back down to the rafts with another harness to bring up the next person.

Jenny was the next one brought up from the raft and then Crystal, followed by Julia.

After the four of them were aboard the chopper, Tim and Roger were pulled up from the rafts.

A few minutes later the three sailors who had jumped into the ocean to help them out of the rafts were aboard the helicopter.

When the woman sailor took off her dive suit, she directed the chopper to take them to the Coast Guard cutter.

Then she announced to the seven rescued passengers, that she was Lt. Commander Serene Sessions, the Captain of the Coast Guard cutter.

Tom was surprised the commander of a Coast Guard cutter would have taken part in their rescue.

She asked, "Are you Tom Parker?"

Tom replied, "Yes, I'm Tom Parker."

Commander Sessions said, "I'm glad you are all right, it seems the CIA was very worried about you and your family.

"When we are back on the cutter, I'm directed to have you call Ron Parsons at CIA Headquarters."

"I'll do that, commander."

Tom thought to himself the sailors assigned to the Coast Guard cutter must enjoy taking orders from someone like Lt. Commander Serene Sessions.

She appeared to be in her late thirties, long blond curly hair, beautiful dark brown eyes, with a body very well put together and about five-foot, eight inches tall.

Tom never remembered having any company commander like her giving orders to him.

Soon after arriving at the Coast Guard cutter and as soon as the chopper was safely on deck, crew members on deck gave six of the seven passengers picked up out of the sea dry clothes and they were taken to quarters below deck to have a chance to warm up and put on the clothes that had been given to them.

They didn't have anything that would fit Tommy, the best they could do was give him a warm blanket to wrap up in.

Jenny told them, Tommy would be fine and thanked them for his blanket.

Tommy didn't seem to mind much, as he enjoyed the warm blanket and the fuss the sailors were making over him.

As soon as Tom had put on the coveralls given him, he asked if Commander Sessions was available, since she said he needed to make a telephone call when he was onboard her ship.

A sailor toldTom he would take him to the bridge, where she was directing their return to base at Kodiak, Alaska.

The sailor took Tom to the bridge of the cutter where Commander Sessions was waiting for him.

She asked him if everyone was all right and if they needed anything.

Tom told her yes, everyone was fine, and he didn't know of anything anyone needed right now.

"He said, "I do need to call Ron Parsons if you have a phone I can use with a little privacy.

Serene replied, "The most privacy we have aboard this ship is in my quarters and you are welcome to use it for your call."

Tom thanked her and she led him to her quarters.

Tom's call to Ron Parsons was put through as soon as the operator knew who was calling.

Ron asked, "Tom, are you and your family all right?"

"Thanks Ron, everyone on board the plane is fine. I don't think anyone even got a scratch, so we are all doing OK."

Ron asked, "Tom what happened to the plane anyway?"

"I'm not sure our pilots have any idea what went wrong with the engines. Everything was fine until they simply shut down, our guys were able to restart the engines once, but they conked out and we went into the ocean."

Ron said, "Do you think someone tampered with the engines and were trying to kill you? You know al-Qaeda has a five- million dollar reward on you, don't you?"

"Yeah, I know it, Ron. Our plane has been taken care of by Cathay Pacific Airlines and parked in their hangar at Los Angeles International Airport."

"Tom, I'm going to have the FBI look into the people who work at that facility.

"One more thing before I let you off the line, Tom. I've been thinking that since we can't keep Jenny from going with you while you're working for the CIA, we're going to have to make her a CIA agent."

"You've got to be kidding!"

"Tom, I've never been more serious in my life. Frankly, if something happened to her while she was with you, I don't have any way of explaining what in the hell she was doing there.

"At least if she got killed or seriously injured, then she's just another CIA agent and we don't have to explain it to anyone."

Tom said, "Great way to cover your ass!"

"Now Tom, you and I both know I have to protect the company and since you can't control your

own wife and make her stay home to take care of your son, the only thing I can do is to make her a CIA agent."

"You know, Ron. I would like for you to try to make her do something she didn't want to do. I'd enjoy that a lot! Next, I'll bet you want me to tell her she has to become a CIA agent to go on this assignment."

"Tom, I'm sure it would be better coming from you than me."

"Oh, I'm quite sure it will."

"Thanks Tom, I knew you would understand, and as soon as I can get any results back from the FBI about what happened to your plane. I'll let you know."

"Good bye, Ron."

Tom went to Jenny and said, "Jenny, my love, you've just gotten a new job."

"What do you mean? I've gotten a new job?"

"Ron Parsons said if you insist on going with me on missions, you have to become a CIA agent."

"Why in the hell would he think I would ever consider becoming a CIA agent?"

"Simple, my darling, if you want to go on missions with me, he has to cover his ass and the only way he can do it is to make you a CIA agent."

"Well what happens if I don't agree to become a CIA agent?"

"Again, it's simple, they won't send me on anymore assignments."

"Now I have a dilemma. If I don't accept becoming a CIA agent you won't be asked to go on any more assignments for them. While I would love not having you in danger all the time, you would hate it, because you know you can help with America's problems but I'm going to hate being a CIA agent.

"One thing you can be sure of: if you're going on an assignments for the CIA. I'm going with you. I guess I don't really have a choice, since I love you and don't want to have you mad at me for the rest of my life. I guess I'm your new CIA agent."

"All right, sweetheart. I'll tell Ron, so he can get the necessary paperwork done and get you your CIA credentials and I do love you so."

Tom reached for Jenny's right hand and pulled her close to him and sweetly kissed her on the lips. Then he told her again how much he loved her.

Tommy had been playing on the floor during the conversation and looked up at his parents and said, "I love my mommy and daddy."

Tom reached down and picked him up and held him between Jenny and himself and said, "We love you too."

As tears ran down Tom's face he knew he had a family, a real family of his own, after all the years he had been alone during his time serving in the army and with the CIA.

For the first time in his adult life he was satisfied being who he was.

Tom returned to the bridge of the cutter to ask Commander Sessions if he could use her quarters to call the CIA again.

Of course she told him he could and after a very short call to Ron Parsons, he returned to Jenny and Tommy.

Tom said, "Jenny, as of right now you're on the payroll of the United States Government as a CIA agent, congratulations, agent Jenny Parker."

"OK, so where's my badge and credentials and do I get a gun too?"

"Ron said he would have them ready for you when we arrive in Hong Kong and you can be sworn in at the American Consulate in Hong Kong.

"I don't think they'll give you a gun though, but maybe I will. Of course, the first thing we have to do is to get to Hong Kong.

"I'll go talk to Commander Sessions about how we can get to Anchorage to get a flight into Hong Kong."

"Tom, I think you should call the fellow you bought the plane from in Los Angeles and see what he can do to get us a new plane, since we'll have to replace the old one. After having our own plane we know we can't get along without having one."

"OK Jenny, I'll try to call C.K. Koontz to see what he can do for us, but it will have to wait until morning since it's getting late tonight and I'm sure their office is closed by now."

Later that night they arrived in Kodiak, Alaska and were given places to stay on the Coast Guard base.

The next morning Tom met with Commander Serene Sessions to thank her and her crew for rescuing them and to ask her how they could get a ride to Anchorage.

Serene told him she would fly them there. One problem solved.

Tom felt she was a very capable and personable commander and asked her how long she had been in the Coast Guard.

She told him since she graduated from the Coast Guard Academy. She said it will soon be twenty years.

He asked if she planned to stay for thirty years and she told him, no, she didn't think so.

"What would you do if you retire?"

She said, "Don't know.

Tom said, "You should think about joining the CIA, they could use someone with your skills."

"I never thought about joining anything like the CIA. I'm not spy material."

"Serene, may I call you that?"

"Certainly, if I can call you, Tom?"

"Not a problem, Serene. The CIA is a lot more than being a spy and I think you have the skills to be of real service to the company."

"How's that?"

"You can command people; you're not afraid to take risks and I believe you can fly many types of airplanes."

"Well, I can fly different types of planes, from choppers to multi-engine planes, and I grew up flying. My dad was a fighter pilot and he taught me to fly before I was old enough to drive a car.

"Some people think I'm too willing to take risks with my life, but I never take risks with other people's lives, if I can help it."

"Serene, when you get closer to your retirement let me know and I'll see what I can do to get you into the CIA. I really believe you would be a natural."

Tom handed her a business card with his cell number and said, "You can call me on this number."

Tom also made a call to C.K. Koontz at his home and asked about purchasing another plane and explained why they needed another one, because the one he sold them was now in the bottom of the Bering Sea.

C.K. told Tom he had a couple of planes that would serve them nicely, one was a Falcon 2000 EX and they had a new Gulfstream 550.

Tom said, "I know our pilots loved the Gulfstream, so I am sure we would rather have another one. Right now we're in Kodiak, Alaska, but the Coast Guard will be taking us to Anchorage later today.

"Is it possible for you to have the plane brought to us in Anchorage today, since we need to get to Hong Kong as soon as possible?"

C.K. Replied, "Sure Tom, we'll have the plane checked over and have it to you sometime tonight. The price is fifty- nine million dollars."

"Thanks, C.K., it will be greatly appreciated and as soon as we get to Hong Kong, Jenny will have the money transferred to you for the plane."

Commander Sessions told Tom she was ready to fly them to Anchorage now and she had a plane ready to go.

Tom made sure all of his people were ready to go and he had them on the tarmac less than fifteen minutes later.

When all were onboard the Coast Guard plane, Commander Sessions took off for Anchorage, and ninety minutes later they were landing at the Anchorage International Airport.

Tom and the rest of his party thanked Commander Sessions again for picking them up out of the ocean and bringing them safely to Anchorage.

Tom told her one more time to think about what he said about working with the CIA after she finished twenty years with the Coast Guard.

She promised she would do that.

They got a couple of taxis to the Courtyard by Marriott and checked in.

Tom told everyone to buy whatever they needed in the way of clothes and personal items, and he would see that they were reimbursed for their cost.

Tom, Jenny and Tommy took another taxi to the nearest shopping center and bought a couple of changes of clothes and several new outfits for Tommy, plus all of the various personal items all of them needed for their daily grooming.

Arriving back at the hotel they decided to rest for the balance of the day or until the pilot arrived with their new plane.

In the meantime, Captain Roger Dean and First Officer Timothy Turpin had been busy filling out accident reports with the FFA Office in Anchorage on the plane crash.

The FFA's only conclusion was engine failure of undetermined cause resulting in the plane crashing, since they had no way of examining the remains of the plane, since it sunk in the Bering Sea.

Captain Dean was very upset losing a plane after all of the years he had been flying. He never had a scratch on any plane he piloted. His safety record was spotless during the twenty plus years he flew for Cathy Pacific.

He told Tom he would really like to know what happened to his engines.

Tom agreed he would like to know that too.

Around seven the next morning the telephone rang in Tom and Jenny's room. Tom answered the phone and a voice said, "Is this Tom Parker?"

"Yes, this is he."

"Mr. Parker my name is Curly Miller and I have your new plane at the fixed base operator's hangar at the Anchorage International Airport and would like to deliver it to you this morning, if that's all right."

"That would be great, it will take us awhile to get everyone rounded up before we can get to the airport. Would around 11 a.m. be OK with you?"

"That sounds good. I'll have breakfast and meet you at the office at the hangar."

Tom called Roger to tell him his new plane was at the airport and said he told the pilot who ferried the plane up from LA, that they would meet him around 11 am.

Roger asked if it was all right with him, if he and his crew went ahead, so they had time to look over the plane to be sure everything was good to go.

Tom told him, certainly, go ahead and get everything looked over so we can be ready to depart as soon as we can.

Tom told Roger the pilot's name who brought the plane up from LA was Curly Miller.

By 11 a.m., Tom, Jenny and Tommy, arrived at the airport and found Roger and crew had already checked over the new plane.

They had even made a few touch and go landings to learn how the plane handled on landings and take offs.

Roger was smiling a broad smile when he saw Tom and said, "She's beautiful. She flies like a dream and landing and take offs are even smoother than the Gulfstream V."

Tom signed the delivery receipt for the plane and gave it to Curly Miller and thanked him for bring the plane from LA.

In the meantime, Roger had the plane fueled and Crystal and Julia had filled the plane with snacks, meals and drinks, so the crew had everything ready to go by the time Tom had finished the paperwork for Curly.

Curly wished them a safe flight and hoped they enjoyed the plane. When the door of the plane closed, Roger cranked up the left engine and after it started and was running smoothly he started the right engine and they were soon rolling down the runway and on their way again to Hong Kong.

Jenny told Tom she really liked the interior of the new plane, it seemed to have more room than the old plane and their son, Tommy was soon down on the floor running his new cars after the plane was at cruising speed and altitude.

This time all of them were sure they would make it to Hong Kong and stay out of the ocean."

Seven hours later they landed in Hong Kong and Jenny called her parents to pick them up when they arrived.

Her parents were waiting for them at the Cathy Pacific hangar when they arrived.

Jenny's parents, Johnny and Amber Lee were relieved to see that no one was hurt after the plane crashed in the Bering Sea.

Amber grabbed Tommy and held him close and covered him with kisses while Johnny was doing the same to Jenny. Then Johnny took Tommy from Amber and she grabbed Jenny in her arms.

Tom stood back at a distance and took in the love fest.

Amber kept telling Jenny you're so lucky, you could have all been killed.

Johnny asked, "Tom, what happened to the plane?"

"Johnny, we don't have any idea, the engines just stopped running. We have no idea what happened to the plane."

Amber said, "Thank God, all of you are safe. Let's get in the car and take you home."

Jenny agreed with her mother and they were soon at Lu Towers, Jenny's building where her penthouse apartment was.

Tom was always happy to be there with its beautiful view of Hong Kong from its perch high on Victoria Peak. The sight from her penthouse had to be one of the greatest views in entire world.

Jenny's first husband certainly knew what he was doing when he planned her apartment.

Tom thought it was too bad he had been killed in a car crash in Vietnam. He was a great planner and developer, but due to his death, Tom was blessed to have Jenny for his wife.

4

After a few days rest in Hong Kong and the opportunity to have Jenny sworn in as a CIA agent at the American Consulate, they were ready to leave for Afghanistan.

Jenny was now a fully vetted CIA agent and was issued her CIA ID and a Beretta Nano 9mm automatic weapon that she was to carry in her purse. She didn't like it, but she promised to do it.

After they left the Consulate Jenny said, "Tommy, what am I going to do with a gun in my purse? You know I don't like guns and I wouldn't know what to do with it."

Tom said, "Jenny, just carry it in your purse to make the CIA happy and if you ever need to use it just point it like you point your finger and slowly pull the trigger."

"You know I could never do that. I'd be too afraid I would shoot the wrong person."

"OK, Jenny, just carry, it in your purse and maybe sometime I might need it to protect us."

When they returned to the penthouse. Tom called Roger to have him get everything ready for the trip the next morning.

They planned to leave at 7:30 a.m. to give them time to arrive in Kabul by late afternoon or early evening.

Tommy was staying with his grandparents the night before they were leaving so Jenny didn't have to get him up early the next morning.

Promptly at 7:30 a.m. their plane departed Hong Kong International Airport for Kabul.

The flight took over eight hours and during the flight Tom and Jenny spent the time discussing the events of the past few days and how they would be able to carry out Tom's mission.

Tom certainly hadn't forgotten what he was asked to do. Kill a turncoat and make it look like al-Qaeda did it.

No small trick, and at the same time, keep the deputy commander of the unit on our side in the battle for Afghanistan.

Ron Parson kept telling him how lucky he was. Tom could only hope his luck was holding for this mission.

Tom and Jenny were met at the airport by someone neither of them expected to see in Kabul. It was Steve Troxler, the head of the CIA in Hong Kong.

Tom said, "Steve Troxler, what in the hell are you doing in Kabul?"

"I guess your old friend, Ron Parsons, thought I had it too soft in Hong Kong. So he sent me here a couple of months ago. So how are the two of you?"

Jenny replied, "We're both fine, just tired after our trip since we lost a plane in the Bering Sea, which I might say wasn't a lot of fun."

"Ron told me about that and he's having the FBI look into the people who serviced your plane in LA. He thinks someone did something to the engines to cause your crash."

Tom said, "I'm sure if Ron is having the FBI look into things, he will get the answers on what happened to our plane."

Steve said, "Yeah, I'd hate to have Ron Parsons looking into my actions against one of his agents.

"The FBI maybe doing the investigation, but you can be sure he will be following every step they make.

"Enough of that, let's get you to somewhere you can get some rest before you head out into the wild country."

Tom asked if Steve thought it was safe to leave their plane in Kabul and the reply was a resounding "No!"

Tom talked to Roger and told him he should take the plane out of Kabul as soon as he and his crew got the plane refueled and a little rest.

He said, "Fly it to Dhabi to keep the plane and the crew safe until we finish our business in Afghanistan."

Tom was sure Roger and his crew would feel a lot safer in Dhabi than waiting around in Kabul for them to finish their job in Afghanistan.

Steve made arrangements to have guards look after the plane for the time it was in Kabul and a place for all of them to sleep and rest for the night.

The next morning Roger and his crew left for Dhabi and Tom and Jenny were scheduled to meet with CIA Agent Harold La Blanc, who in turn would introduce them to al-Garde.

Tom knew this part would go OK. He just didn't have any idea where to go from there.

At ten o'clock Steve and Harold La Blanc arrived to talk with Tom and Jenny.

After the introductions, Tom asked what Harold thought about al Garde, in light of the gun battle resulting in the deaths of seven American soldiers.

Harold curtly replied. "I think Washington is making far too much of this accident, that's what I think!"

Tom said, "Why do you think that, Harold? We lost seven Americans."

"Because it was an accident, we've lost a lot more men than that due to friendly fire. That's all that happened here, friendly fire."

"Well, Harold, it's friendly fire as long as it's killing some other American. If you're one of those who got shot, you wouldn't think the fire was very friendly."

"What if I told you I don't believe it? I think your Mr. al-Garde has turned on you and you don't even know it!"

"Bullshit! I'd trust my life on al-Garde; he's with us all the way!"

Tom said, "Well, from what I've heard, I wouldn't trust him any farther than I could throw a platoon of overweight marines!"

Harold calmed down a little before he replied to Tom then said, "Mr. Parker, maybe you are right, maybe I've been with him too much to believe that he's turned on us."

"Listen Harold, if you're wrong about him, then he could cost us a lot of good men and if you're right we could be losing a great ally.

"No matter what you were told, the reason I'm here is to help you make that decision."

"All right, Parker, how do you plan to do this?"

"Good question, Harold, but I don't have a good answer for it right now."

"Well if you don't know how we're going to do it, what do you want me to do?"

"The best thing you can do is to rejoin al-Garde and his men and let him know that some old retired army colonel has been sent by the Pentagon to look into the deaths of the seven soldiers."

"Assure al-Garde, it's just routine and that the army always sends out someone to file a report so it looks to the parents of the men killed that the army really cared about their loved ones."

Three days later, Tom met up with Harold and al- Garde and his men somewhere southwest of Kabul.

Tom had a hard time getting Jenny to stay in Kabul, while he went to meet with Harold and al-Garde, but he promised to return the next day.

Jenny had some work she needed to finish for Lu Investments, so she reluctantly agreed to stay behind for one night, but only one night.

When Harold introduced Tom to al-Garde. Tom could tell al-Garde sensed Tom could be a threat to him, just by the way al-Garde never looked Tom in the eye and by his posture.

There was no doubt in Tom's mind that al-Garde was in a defensive mode.

Al-Garde's voice certainly never indicated the things Tom saw and sensed; in fact, he was overly friendly and pleasant.

Tom now understood why Harold doubted al-Garde was anything but on our side.

Tom thought he would have to judge al-Garde himself, as he had been forced to do over the years and dealing with all types of people all over the world.

Al-Garde said, "Colonel Parker, I want you to know how sorry I am about ambushing those American troops, we simply had the wrong information."

"It was a dreadful mistake and my men and I are very sorry about it."

"Commander al-Garde, I know sometimes in the heat of battle things go wrong and the army has sent me here to get a better understanding of what went wrong and make suggestions to try to prevent it from happening again."

"Colonel Parker, I'm so glad they sent a professional solider with combat experience to investigate this situation, and I would like to give you all of the information I know about it right now."

"Commander, I'm sorry, but I'm not really up to taking your deposition tonight although you speak excellent English.

"I do have a translator coming tomorrow to help me if you or your men aren't comfortable testifying in English for the record."

"Colonel, I didn't understand there would be a formal hearing on this problem."

"Well, commander, anytime seven American soldiers are killed by some of our troops or people working with us, it has to be investigated to be sure there was no wrong doing or someone caused these men to be killed on purpose. I'm sure you can understand that."

"OK, sure I understand it now, tomorrow then. I'll say goodnight now."

"Thank you for understanding, commander. I'll see you in the morning."

Al-Garde walked away in a huff. Tom could plainly see he was upset with the idea of giving a formal deposition about the killing of the seven American soldiers, which was exactly the reaction Tom wanted to see and he did.

Harold showed Tom to a tent that he could have for the night, but asked Tom, "Why did you tell al-Garde you had a translator coming in the morning and planned to take his and the rest of his troops deposition?"

"I wanted to see how he would react, and for an innocent man he reacted pretty badly. I would say right now, I think al-Garde knew who his men and he were attacking. "

Harold replied, "I just can't believe it."

"I'm sorry, Harold, but I think your man has turned on you."

"Goodnight, Colonel Parker. I'll see you in the morning."

Harold left the tent in almost the same huff that al- Garde had left a few minutes ago.

Tom got himself ready for a night's sleep, but he was concerned he might be attacked by al-Garde or one of his men, so instead of lying down on the bed next to the sidewall of the tent. He folded up some blankets and placed them on the bed.

He made a bed on the floor of the tent using only a blanket and a pillow and under his pillow he placed his 9 millimeter pistol.

Tom's gut feeling turned out to be right as it had been so many times before.

Around three a.m., Tom heard a knife blade cutting through the sidewall of his tent and as he rose up from his blanket. He saw an arm strike down toward his bed and as the knife blade struck the empty bed, Tom fired his weapon and fired once more, as he saw a man's body fall against the wall of the tent.

Tom quickly raced out of the tent and saw someone running away from his tent. The person running saw Tom and he turned and fired a shot at him before Tom could fire his weapon.

Tom felt a sudden pain in his right shoulder that caused him to fall to the ground and drop his pistol.

The man kept running into the dark as Tom found his weapon. Using his left hand to hold the pistol, he fired once more at the man.

The man fell to the ground but managed to get up and then fell again. Then Tom saw someone else helping to pull up the wounded man and into a waiting vehicle and it rapidly pulled away, leaving Tom lying on the ground where he had fallen.

By this time the camp was ablaze with lights and people scrambling in all directions to ward off the attackers.

Harold rushed to Tom's tent and first found the man Tom had shot laying half in and half out of the tent.

Next, he found Tom who was sitting up holding something on his wounded shoulder,

Harold shouted to have a medic come to help Tom and by this time several of al-Garde's men had gathered around Tom.

A medic arrived and asked Harold to help Tom into the tent where Tom could lay down on the bed.

Two men helped Tom to his feet and steady him as he walked back inside his tent.

The medic had gone ahead and checked over the man Tom had shot and said he was dead.

Men outside the tent moved the man's body away from the tent and were surprised to find it was one of al-Garde's personal bodyguards.

The medic looked over Tom's wound and told him he was lucky, since the bullet had gone straight through his shoulder missing the bone, but it had torn through several muscles and might need to be repaired by a surgeon.

The medic assured Tom, the army has some very good surgeons in Kabul, who could take care of his shoulder.

In the meantime, the medic gave Tom a shot for the pain and cleaned and bandaged up the wound.

Tom asked Harold to check the camp to see who was missing.

Harold came back a few minutes later and informed Tom, al-Garde and his other personal bodyguard were gone with their vehicle.

Tom asked Harold to ask al-Mazano to come to his tent before he left for Kabul.

A few minutes passed before Harold returned with al- Mazano. After being introduced, Tom asked al-Mazano if he knew why al-Garde and his men wanted to kill him.

Al-Mazano told Tom he had no idea, but he said al- Garde had been acting very strange since he ordered the attack on the American soldiers, but thought it was caused by him making a mistake. Now he said he thought it wasn't a mistake and he intended to kill those men.

Tom said, "I know you have many good men who want to help rid your country of al- Qaeda and Taliban. Do you think you can take control of the men that you have now since al-Garde has left you?"

Al-Mazano heisted for a few minutes before answering and then said, "Yes, Colonel Parker. I believe I can."

"That's good, very good. America needs you and your men to help us rid your country of these people once and forever, thank you, Commander al-Mazano."

"Thank you, Colonel Parker, for believing in me."

"I think I'd better get to Kabul to the hospital as soon as I can."

After saying that, Tom lay down on his bed and went to sleep, aided by the shot given to him by the medic for his pain and the need for sleep.

5

Tom woke up when they were taking him out of the back of an Army Ambulance in Kabul and much to his surprise, the second person he saw was Jenny. Jenny said, "Tom, are you OK, how badly are you hurt? I knew I should never have let you go without me being with you."

Tom replied, "I am sure I'll be all right, just got a bullet in my right shoulder, that's all."

A nurse told Jenny, "Mrs. Parker, we need to take your husband into surgery right now, but I'm sure he will be fine." Tom said, "Jenny, you can come with me until we get to the surgery operating room, take my left hand, my love." Jenny reached and took hold of Tom's left hand as two orderlies began to move Tom's cart to an elevator to take him up to the operating room.

Jenny held Tom's hand until they were trying to get his gurney through the elevator door, then she got into the elevator and took Tom's hand again until they reached the surgical floor.

Again Jenny had to release Tom's hand to let the orderlies get Tom's gurney out of the elevator.

As soon as they had his gurney out of the elevator, she had Tom's hand in hers until they came to the door of the operating room.

Then one of the orderlies said, "Mrs. Parker, please give your husband a kiss goodbye, because we need to get him into the operating room."

Jenny leaned down and gave Tom a kiss and said, "I'm not giving you a goodbye kiss, only a little kiss to let you know I love you and I expect you to get well quickly."

After Jenny kissed him, Tom said, "No, that wasn't a goodbye kiss, just a little I'll-see-you-soon kiss."

Then the orderlies wheeled his gurney into the operating room.

A nurse gave Tom a shot for pain before the orderlies transferred him from the gurney to an operating table.

A doctor said, "Colonel Parker, I am going to be giving you something to help you relax and go to sleep now.

The anesthesiologist placed a needle into the intravenous line on the back of Tom's left hand, which was strapped to Tom's wrist to prevent movement of the needle being inserted.

As the anesthetic was being given to Tom, the anesthesiologist asked Tom to start counting down from one hundred.

Tom started counting: one hundred; ninety-nine; ninety-eight; ninety-seven; ninety-six.

No more counting. Tom was out.

The army surgeon made an incision into Tom's right shoulder and began to access the damage caused by the bullet passing through Tom's right shoulder.

The surgeon found the bullet passed through the shoulder missing the shoulder blade by less than an inch, but required repairing the pectoral major muscle that lifts the shoulder.

The surgery took a little over an hour and Jenny was becoming very anxious over the amount of time the surgery was taking. Maybe Tom was hurt worse than the doctors thought he was.

She was getting ready to try to find someone to ask about how Tom's surgery was coming, when a young doctor came up to her in the surgery waiting area and asked if she was Mrs. Parker.

She told the doctor she was Mrs. Parker.

The doctor said, "Mrs. Parker, everything went fine with Tom's surgery, he has been taken to the recovery room and next we will move him into a private room."

Jenny asked, "How bad is Tom's wound?"

"I would say he will have complete recovery in about three or four months, maybe less. He will have to go through some extended period of rehabilitation, meaning lots of exercises, to get full usage of his right arm and hand.

"To begin with we will have him in a cast to restrict movement of his shoulder and right arm.

"I can't say how long we may have to keep his shoulder and arm in a cast. Right now it will depend on how quickly he heals from the surgery.

"You will be allowed to see Tom in the recovery room after we are sure we have him stable.

"If you like, I will take you to the recovery room waiting area and when we're sure Tom is stable, someone will come and get you and take you to see him."

"Thank you, doctor. I would appreciate that."

The doctor said, "All right, Mrs. Parker, please follow me."

Jenny got up from her chair and began to follow the young doctor.

He soon led her to the recovery room waiting area and said, "OK, Mrs. Parker, just wait here and someone will be out to take you to your husband as soon as he is stable."

Jenny took a seat in one of the chairs in the waiting area as the doctor went into the recovery room.

Time passed slowly as it always does when you are waiting for some news about a loved one in a hospital.

Jenny looked around and saw she was the only person in the recovery room waiting area.

Jenny quickly came to the conclusion the reason no one else was here waiting for news of a loved one was because none of the military patients having surgery had family in Afghanistan.

An hour passed before a nurse came out of the recovery room and said, "Mrs. Parker, your husband is asking for you. Would you please come with me?'

Jenny replied, "Yes, I was hoping I'd get to see Tom before too much more time went by."

Jenny rose from her chair and followed the nurse into the recovery room.

Arriving there Jenny saw Tom was awake and had his head turned to the doorway watching for Jenny to come in.

Jenny said, "How are you, my love?"

"Can't you tell? I'm doing great. My shoulder is a little banged up but otherwise, I'm OK."

"You look like you could use a kiss to make you feel better."

"I'm sure that would help."

Jenny leaned down and kissed Tom lightly on the lips.

Then she said, "Sorry, solider, that's the best I can do right now."

Tom replied, "I guess I have to get better to get a better kiss."

A nurse said, "Colonel, we have a room ready for you now and I'll have an orderly take you to your room when you're ready."

"OK, nurse, I am ready when your orderly is ready."

"He will be here in just a few minutes. Mrs. Parker, if you like you may wait here and go with them so you know where your husband's room will be."

"Thank you, nurse, I'll do that."

Only a few minutes passed before an orderly arrived and said, "Colonel Parker, are you ready to take a little ride?"

"Whenever you're ready. I'll ride along with you since you're driving."

The orderly begin pushing Tom's bed out of the recovery room through the door and down the long hallway.

Jenny followed behind the orderly who pushed Tom's bed out of the recovery room door and down the hallway.

It seemed like they were going on a long walk and then the orderly stopped and opened a door at room 420.

The orderly opened the door as wide as he could and then pushed Tom's bed into the room.

Jenny followed them into Tom's room and watched as the orderly locked the wheels of the bed, so it would stay in place. Then the orderly helped Tom move into his bed.

Just as the orderly was finishing helping Tom into his bed a nurse came into the room and said, "Colonel Parker, how are you doing after your long bed ride?"

Tom replied, "I doing OK. My driver did a fine job driving me here and getting me into bed."

The orderly said, "Thank you, colonel. Hope you are soon out of here and doing OK."

"Thanks.'

The orderly left as the nurse begin to check Tom's vital signs.

She checked his pulse, temperature and blood pressure and listened to his heart.

After she finished making her checks she asked, "How are you feeling, colonel?"

"I'm doing all right, just have some pain in my shoulder, but it's not too bad."

The nurse asked him if he would like something to drink or eat.

Tom told her, no, not at this time. I just want to rest for a while.

She said, "OK, we'll let you rest for now, however if you need anything, just let us know, OK?"

"Thank you, nurse."

Then the nurse asked Jenny if she needed anything to eat or drink.

Jenny said, "No, I just want to be here with my husband."

"OK, I leave you two alone. We will check on both of you later."

Then the nurse left the room leaving Tom and Jenny alone.

Tom soon fell asleep and Jenny sat in her chair across the room.

Soon it was getting dark and Tom continued to sleep. Nurses kept coming into the room every hour or so and Tom hardly acknowledged them taking his vital signs.

About nine o'clock that night, the nurse asked Jenny if she could bring her something to eat and drink since, she hadn't had anything to eat all day.

A few minutes passed and an aide brought her a ham and cheese sandwich, potato salad and a large coke.

Jenny thanked the woman and soon ate everything they brought her and finished her coke. She felt better and had no plans to leave Tom alone tonight.

Around midnight a nurse came to the room and checked Tom's vital signs and told Jenny everything with Tom was OK, and told Jenny she should try to get some rest.

Jenny turned off the lights in the room except a night light that was under Tom's bed and she curled up in a chair with her purse on her lap to see if she could get some sleep.

She was trying to get some sleep when a man in a janitor's uniform came into the room with a mop and a cleaning cart.

He couldn't see Jenny sitting on the other side of the room in the dark.

He was looking at Tom lying sleeping and Jenny saw the man take something out of his cleaning bag and she saw a knife blade flash from the light from under the Tom's bed.

The man cautiously approached Tom's bed and raised the knife and Jenny said, "What are you doing?"

The man turned to Jenny and started walking toward her and Jenny quickly opened her purse and took out the

Beretta 9mm, when the man raised his hand with his knife to strike her.

Jenny remembered what Tom had told her about her gun. She pointed the barrel of the gun like it was her finger and pulled the trigger of her weapon.

The bullet hit the man in the chest and he stumbled onto the floor but the man tried to get up and was swinging his knife at Jenny.

Jenny pulled the trigger of the Beretta two more times and the man fell at her feet.

The noise from the gunshots rang out loudly in the quiet hospital.

Tom woke up and was getting out of bed when several nurses and aides rushed into Tom's room, turned on the lights and saw the man lying on the floor in front of Jenny and Jenny still holding the Beretta in her hand.

Soon MPs came running into Tom's room and saw the dead man lying at Jenny's feet and the knife blade stuck into Jenny's pant leg.

Jenny put the Beretta back into her purse. By that time, Tom was out of his bed standing next to Jenny.

Tom asked Jenny if she was all right and she calmly said, "Yes, I am all right, that man was trying to kill you."

A nurse or an aide brought a wheelchair in and asked Tom to please sit down.

Tom did as he was asked to do and the MP asked Jenny if she could tell them what happened.

Jenny said, "I was trying to get some rest and I saw this man come into the room and I thought he was going to clean the room, but then I saw him take a knife out of the cleaning bag and the knife blade flashed in the night light.

"I asked him what he was doing. He hadn't seen me in the chair, because I was sitting in the dark, then he started toward me with the knife raised to strike me.

"I pulled the gun out of my purse and shot him, but he kept coming at me so I fired two more shots at him and he fell to the floor."

Tom said, "Jenny did he hurt your leg?"

Jenny replied, "I don't think so."

The MP reached down and pulled the knife out of Jenny's pant leg. Then he raised her pant leg up and saw a cut on her leg which was bleeding.

One of the nurses quickly attended to Jenny's leg and cleaned the wound and put a bandage on her leg.

They turned the man's body over but no one knew who the man was. He was not someone who worked in the hospital.

They soon checked and found the body of the janitor who was supposed to be working on the floor cleaning rooms, his throat had been cut.

The captain of the MPs asked Jenny why she had a gun in her purse.

She told him because the CIA insists that I carry a gun, because I'm a CIA agent. Jenny took her CIA ID and showed it to the captain, he looked at it and handed it back to her and said, "Thank you."

Then he said, "You know, you saved your husband's life tonight."

Tom said, "Yes, you did, thank you, my love."

"You are very welcome, my love."

Tom's nurse said, "We need to get you back to bed, colonel. We will move you to a room right across the hall, if that's OK with you and your wife?"

Tom replied, "Thank you, that will be fine, don't you agree Jenny?"

"Yes, the sooner the better."

The nurse pushed Tom's wheelchair across the hall to a new room with Jenny following right behind them.

After the nurse helped Tom get back into bed, she asked him if he needed anything else and he told her, no, he was all right.

When the nurse left the room Jenny came to Tom's bedside and said, "Tommy, I remembered what you told me to do with the gun. I just pointed the gun at the man with the knife and pulled the trigger on the gun and when he kept coming at me with his knife, I pulled the trigger two more times and he fell to the floor."

"I know, sweetheart, you saved both of our lives, thank you."

"Did I really do that?"

"Yes, you did and I'm so proud of you."

"Tommy, I think I'm going to faint."

"No, you're not going to faint, just lie down beside me on this bed and let me hold you."

Jenny did lie down next to Tommy and he held her as close as he could. Jenny relaxed and both of them were soon asleep.

After everyone left the room the MPs had a doctor come into Tom's old room and check the man's body and he confirmed the man was dead, killed by being shot in the chest three times with 9mm bullets.

They didn't find any identification on the man's body.

So they had no idea what to do with his body.

They decided to turn his body over to the local police to see if anyone would claim his body.

If someone did, maybe they would have an idea who the man was and why he wanted to kill Tom Parker.

6

Tom and Jenny both woke up the next morning when a nurse came into their room and asked, "How are you two doing this morning?"

Tom replied, "I'm doing a lot better than I was when I came in here yesterday. I'm not having as much pain in my shoulder."

Jenny woke up after hearing Tom speak and tried to quickly get up off of Tom's bed.

The nurse said, "It's OK, Mrs. Parker, the whole hospital is buzzing about how you saved your husband's and your life last night. None of us had any idea you were a CIA agent. We think you should get a medal or something for your quick actions.

"Let me check your leg to make sure it's healing OK, then I'll get the colonel's vitals."

Jenny got off of Tom's bed and the nurse pointed at a chair for her to sit down on, so she could check Jenny's leg.

The nurse took the bandage off and saw her wound was still spotting blood.

The nurse told Jenny she would be right back and redress her wounded leg from that nasty old knife cut.

The nurse asked, "Mrs. Parker, do you need something for pain, is it hurting you too much?"

Jenny replied, "No, it's not too bad, but maybe if I could have a couple of aspirin, it might help me with my pain."

The nurse told Jenny she would be right back and she would redress her leg and bring her some aspirin.

Tom said as soon as the nurse was gone, "Well, Jenny, it looks like you have become a hero killing that man last night and saving my life."

Jenny replied, "I don't feel like a hero, I'm just glad both of us are still alive."

Tom got out of bed and came over to where Jenny was sitting and gave her a big kiss and said, "Good morning, my darling, you will always be my hero."

"Thanks."

By that time the nurse had returned with two aspirin and the items she needed to redress Jenny's wounded leg.

Tom got Jenny a glass of water and handed it to her to be able to take her aspirin while the nurse was cleaning the wound on Jenny's leg and putting on a new bandage.

When the nurse was finished dressing Jenny's leg she said, "OK, Colonel Parker, it's your turn, let's see how you are doing today.

"Would you please get back in bed so I can take your vital signs?"

Tom did as the nurse asked and got into his bed.

The nurse checked Tom's blood pressure, temperature and his heart rate.

When she was finished she said, "Everything is looking great, colonel."

Next, she checked around his cast to see if it had stayed in place and it looked like it was OK.

"Everything is looking good, colonel."

"Nurse, do you know how long they are planning on keeping me in the hospital?"

"I'm sorry, colonel. I don't have any idea, normally with your gunshot wound they would be keeping you until that cast was ready to come off and then have you stay and do rehab to make sure everything with your shoulder and arm were working all right."

"Thank you, nurse, would you ask my doctor to come and see me as soon as he can?

"I will do that, colonel, I know he's in surgery at this time. We had three wounded men come in early this morning and he is doing surgery on two of them. I sorry to say, we lost the third man."

"I'm really sorry to hear about you losing one of the men."

"Yes sir, colonel, we're all really sorry every time we lose anyone, it breaks our hearts. If they make it to our hospital, we don't lose very many of them, so it really tears us all up when we fail one."

"Thank you, nurse, how long have you been here?"

"It seems like forever, but it's really only a little over a year. They try to rotate us out every year, but sometimes they don't have enough people so we're here a little longer.

"This is my fourth tour of duty here."

"Thanks for all your help with my wife and myself. I wanted to tell you it was certainly appreciated.

"Thank you, colonel, for the kind words and I know you've had more than your share of wounds, looking at your army medical records.

"They will be bringing both of you some breakfast in a few minutes and plenty of hot coffee for you, colonel, and hot tea for madam.

"It's been a real pleasure meeting both of you and I hope you can get out of here very soon."

"It was about four o'clock in the afternoon before Tom's doctor came to see him.

When he arrived in Tom's room he said, "Sorry to be so long before I could come to see you, colonel, but I just finished in the operating room."

Tom said, "I understand it has been a rough day for you, doctor, so how are your patients doing?

"I'm sorry to say we lost the first one we were working on, he was just too badly wounded for us to be of much help. We did everything we could to save our eighteen- year-old soldier, but our efforts were just not enough."

Tom and Jenny could see tears forming in the doctor's eyes as he talked about losing this young man.

Tom said, "Doc, you can do no more than your best and sometime even the best is not enough.

"I lost a lot of men over my years in service. Some of my best friends died in my arms, really too many to talk about. If there is anyone in the world who understands what you are going through, it's me.

"Sorry doc, you learn you can't save them all, all you can do is keep trying your best and with God's will, save as many as them as you can."

"Thanks, Colonel Parker, I needed to hear that. I keep thinking about my own son who will soon be coming into

the army and I don't know how I would handle it if I lost him in some war."

"Well, doc, in the old days we would have said, just have girls, but that's not much help these days, the girls are right there fighting with our sons.

"Just one last word of advice, just keep doing your best and keep remembering all the soldiers you saved, feel bad about the ones you lost, but keep saving as many as you can.

"One more thing before you get away, how soon can you let me out of this hospital, we need to get back to our assignment?"

"Well, colonel, the protocol for your type of wound would be that you can't be checked out of the hospital until we can take your cast off and send you through rehab to be sure your shoulder and arm have healed up properly.

"However, I know we will never be able to hold you here that long, so how about you staying here another three of four days."

"Thanks doctor, if we don't get back on our assignment you might have a lot more casualties to deal with."

"OK, I understand. I will get you out of here as soon as I think it's safe for you to leave, but not one minute more than that."

"Thank you, doctor, you keep caring and saving our people, got it?"

"Yes sir, colonel."

The doctor left the room and Tom said, "I know exactly how the doctor is feeling, I've been there too many times."

Jenny said, "I'm sorry for the doctor and I had no idea of how much you had gone through serving in the army and being a CIA agent.

"Seeing the doctor. I certainly understand you much better and what you have been through. Tommy, you've had a tough life and doing it all on your own must have been really hard not to have someone who loved you that you could share it with.

"Sorry, I wasn't there for you."

"It's OK, Jenny, you're here now. We have to get out of this hospital and finish our assignment. We have to find and kill al-Garde."

The telephone in Tom's room rang and Jenny handed the phone to Tom and he answered, "Tom Parker."

The voice of the other end of the line said, "Tom Parker, this is al-Garde. I just want to tell you to get out of Afghanistan, we won't miss you the next time."

Then the phone went dead.

Tom said, "That guy has got some nerve calling me and telling me to get out of Afghanistan."

Jenny asked, "What guy is telling you to get out of Afghanistan?"

"Al-Garde!"

"Tom, you mean he called you in the U.S. Army Hospital and told you to get out of Afghanistan?"

"Yes Jenny, that's who was on the phone."

"In all the years working for the CIA, have you ever had someone tell you to leave their country?"

"No, he's the first one, but it tells me one thing. We can't stay in this hospital, it's too dangerous for us to stay where he knows where we are.

"We've got to get out of here today."

"Jenny, go tell the nurse I need my clothes and we are leaving the hospital as soon as we can.

"I'll call Steve Troxler and ask him to make arrangements to get us out of this hospital as soon as possible."

Jenny left the room to find someone to get some clothes for Tom.

She talked with the nurse who was the shift supervisor and told her that Tom needed to get some clothes, because they had to leave the hospital as soon as they could.

The supervisor said, "I'm sorry, but Colonel Parker can't leave the hospital until his doctor releases him."

Jenny replied, "I'm sorry but it's imperative that we leave the hospital as quickly as we can, my husband just got a threatening telephone call on his life."

The supervisor said, "Do you think he can't be protected here in the hospital?"

Jenny replied, "After last night, no, I don't think he can be. We were lucky once, but I wouldn't want to chance it again.

"OK, Mrs. Parker I'll see if we can find him some clothes and I will contact his doctor to see if he will sign him out of the hospital."

"Thank you, I will go back to his room and wait for you to bring him some clothes and help him get dressed so we can leave as soon as we can."

Jenny returned to Tom's room as Tom was hanging up the telephone.

Tom said, "Jenny, I just finished talking with Steve Troxler and he said he would be here in about twenty minutes to move us to a safer place."

"Tom, the nurse supervisor said she would get you some clothes to wear and talk to the doctor about signing you out of the hospital."

"Good, I hope she can get me something to wear so we can be ready to leave as soon as Steve gets here."

One of the aides came into Tom's room carrying some underwear, socks, fatigue shirt and pants and his own shoes, the ones he was wearing when he arrived at the hospital.

She also brought a fatigue heavy jacket and a cap.

The aide said, "Sir, may I help you get dressed?"

Tom replied, "Yes, please do. I think you have more experience helping wounded soldiers dress than my wife."

"Yes sir, I'm sure I have, since I've been doing it for over ten years.

Getting Tom's hospital gown off and his undershorts on wasn't much trouble or his socks and his pants and shoes, but the aide had a tougher time getting on his fatigue shirt and his fatigue jacket with his shoulder and arm in a cast.

The best they could do was to just kind of wrap the shirt and jacket around his shoulder and right arm.

The aide said she would get a bandage and pull it around the jacket which would at least hold the jacket and shirt tight around Tom.

She got one of the bandages that would just fasten onto itself and hold both pieces of his clothes shut.

She had just finished getting Tom dressed and Steve Troxler and four other men arrived in his room.

Steve said, "We are here to take you to a safe house away from the city and where you can be as well protected in Afghanistan as you can ever be."

Just as Steve finished saying that the nurse supervisor came into Tom's room and said, "I've talked with your doctor and he has signed your release and asked me to give you these pain pills to take with you and he would like to see you again sometime next week if you can come back to the hospital."

Tom thanked her and took the pills she handed him and then gave them to Jenny to put in her purse.

Steve said, "OK, let's get you two out of here."

The aide said, "Colonel Parker, please get into the wheelchair and if you other folks will follow me. I will take you down to your vehicles."

The aide soon had them in an elevator used only by the hospital staff and she showed them were Tom could be put in a vehicle without going outside.

Steve asked one of the men with him to please go get the vehicle they brought to transport Tom and Jenny.

A few minutes later the man brought in an old Land Rover that had four rear wheels and was extra-long in length.

Steve said, "This vehicle was once used by an English planter in India. It's equipped with a bomb-proof body and bullet-proof shaded windows, so it should keep you both safe during our trip."

They helped Tom get into the vehicle and had him sit in a middle row of the vehicle, since the vehicle had three rows of seats.

Jenny got in next to Tom and the rest of Steve's men got into the vehicle, with Steve in the front seat with the driver and they were off.

Tom asked, "Steve, where are you taking Jenny and me?"

Steve said, "We're taking you to an old friend that Jack Hayes introduced you to, Warlord Omar Hekmatyar.

"Omar has become one of our best allies in Afghanistan since he rescued Jack from al-Qaeda and you pinned on his medal."

"I'd guess the twenty-five million dollars we paid him helped a little for turning over Dr. Robert Chew and his men."

"Tom, he's done a lot more since then to help us and, yes, we pay him for his help, but he has done so many things to help us.

"He certainly remembers you and your wife, and always asks about you. When I asked him to protect you until you recovered from your wound, he was happy to have the opportunity to see you both again and promised no one would harm you while you were under his protection."

"You know, Steve, that's not saying a lot for the US forces we have in Afghanistan, if you have to rely on a local warlord to protect us."

"Well, I can tell you the people who live in his kingdom are all fiercely loyal and if they weren't, they would either be gone or dead.

"His people love him and they are taking better care of him than the government could ever do."

"OK, Steve, I believe you."

"One more thing about Omar, he is far more sophisticated and speaks much better English than when you first met him.

"He was never stupid, but he hired a former English officer to work for him and Omar is a far different person today than the man you met when he turned Jack Hayes over to us.

Jenny said, "Well I can't wait to meet this new Omar Hekmatyar."

Steve replied, "Jenny, you will be surprised."

7

Two hours later they arrived at the castle where Omar Hekmatyar lived.

As soon as they arrived they were met by six men with automatic weapons and taken directly to see Omar Hekmatyar.

When they arrived in Omar's office, a secretary bid them welcome in English and said, "Warlord Omar, will see you soon.

"He has been in a meeting with some of the security forces who will be looking out for our guests.

"Please have a seat and I will let Warlord Omar know you have arrived."

Tom, Jenny and Steve took seats on some very nice- looking leather chairs.

The secretary picked up a telephone and they heard her say something in a language they couldn't understand.

She hung up the telephone and said, "Warlord Omar said he would be with you in a few minutes."

Only about two minutes passed when his office door opened and a well-dressed man in a business suit said, "Good afternoon, I'm Colonel John Strong, Warlord Omar's military adviser, won't you please come in."

Steve, Tom and Jenny all got up from their chairs and followed Colonel Strong into Omar's office.

Inside the office, Omar got up from behind his desk and went around the desk to meet them.

Tom looked at Warlord Omar and couldn't believe it was the same man that he met when he had turned Jack over to him.

Omar was still as tall, but he must have lost more than one hundred pounds and was dressed in what was like a military uniform with gold braid on the cuffs of his sleeves and with the crest on his left chest and his bronze star on his right chest.

His hair and beard were nicely trimmed and he looked like he was twenty years younger than when Tom saw him last.

He greeted Tom first and said, "Colonel Tom Parker, how are you doing. I understand you were recently wounded by a traitor to our cause. I hope your wounds are not causing you too much pain."

"No. Warlord Omar, they're not too bad. I appreciate you agreeing to have us as your guests until I can recover a little."

"On the contrary, I appreciate having the opportunity to see you and meet your lovely wife. We will do everything possible to keep you safe and comfortable during your stay.

"If there is anything you want or need, just tell us and it will be done.

"Mrs. Parker, how are you holding up during this trying time for you and your husband?"

"Thank you, I'm doing just fine."

"I glad you are doing OK, Mrs. Parker. I understand you had to kill a man who was trying to kill your husband in the hospital.

"I am really sorry to hear that. I am sure it must have been awful experience for you."

"Well, the man didn't give me much of a choice, since he was trying to kill me too."

"Let me show you to your rooms. I'm sure after the night you had last night and then traveling here today, you both must need some time to rest before dinner."

Tom said, "That would be greatly appreciated. I am pretty tired right now and having an opportunity to lie down for a while would be wonderful."

Steve said, "Warlord Omar, I'm going to excuse myself because I need to get back to Kabul tonight.

"So I will see you in a week or so, when I come back to pick up Tom and Jenny."

"I am sorry you can't stay overnight, but I will say goodbye for now and see you when you return for my guests."

Steve left to go back to Kabul as Warlord Omar was showing Tom and Jenny to their rooms.

Tom and Jenny were very impressed when they arrived at their quarters; they had a sitting room which looked as if it had never been used before, a large bedroom with a king-size bed and a lovely modern bathroom complete with double sinks, bathtub, shower, bidet and toilet stool.

There were even plenty of large soft towels and face cloths. Shampoo and body lotion and bars of soap were provided in the bathroom.

Everything was clean, modern and beautiful in their rooms. They even had a coffee pot and a small refrigerator, stocked with soft drinks and bottled water from the USA.

Omar had thought of everything for his guests.

Omar told them if they needed anything to just ring the bell next to the bed or couch and a maid would come to help them, and she spoke some English but she understood it better than she spoke it

Before he left their rooms. Omar said, "Please just call me, Omar. Dinner will be at eight and your maid will bring you to the dining room."

He left and Tom said, "I can't believe that is the same man who brought Jack Hayes to us. He certainly has learned English and manners and as Steve said, he's become very sophisticated and polished.

"What do you think, Jenny, do you think that British Colonel could have had that much influence on Omar?"

"I don't know but someone has, he's a totally different man from the man you saw when he brought Jack to us. It's unbelievable, totally unbelievable."

Jenny turned the bed covers down as Tom was getting undressed.

As soon as Tom had his pants off and Jenny took his shirt off, he laid down on the bed and was asleep almost before his head hit the pillow.

Jenny took a good look around their bedroom suite and discovered it had everything a five star hotel suite would have, plus many things a hotel wouldn't have.

She found beautiful plush robes and slippers; Champagne cooling in the fridge with Champagne glasses in a special cooler next to the fridge; snacks of all kinds; a TV with special Internet connections to be able to view news from all around the world, such as BBC, CNN, FOX, a Chinese news station and ESPN Sports stations.

After looking around the room she began to feel very tired herself after the hectic night and the trip to Warlord Omar's Castle.

So, she got into bed, next to Tom and was also soon fast asleep.

Jenny woke up and found Tom lying next to her and she thought Tom was still trying to keep her close to protect her. She loved him so much.

She looked at her watch and saw it was six-thirty and thought she should wake Tom, so he would have time to get ready for dinner at eight.

When Jenny pulled herself away from Tom he woke up and asked, "What time is it?"

"A little after six-thirty."

"OK, I guess I better get up and try to find something to wear for dinner."

Jenny replied, "I looked around the suite, but didn't find any clothes except what we had on when we arrived here."

Jenny got out of bed and saw a door that might be a closet. She hadn't opened that door during her time exploring the suite.

Jenny opened this door as Tom was sliding out of bed and Jenny saw their luggage was in the closet and placed on luggage racks.

Jenny said, "Tommy, I guess someone brought our luggage here from Kabul and placed it in the closet for us."

Tom replied, "Thanks to whoever brought our things to us. I am going to take a quick shower and find something to wear for dinner. I hope Omar's not dressing in formal dining gear tonight."

Jenny laughed and replied, "Well, if he does. I guess he will outshine us tonight."

"My darling Jenny, Omar nor anyone else could possibly outshine you, my love, even if you were dressed in a feed sack."

"Tommy, you are just blind with love. My sweet darling, these days too many people can certainly outclass me. I'm getting old you know."

"Old? No, you are just perfect and will always be."

"Thank you, my dear, but get your shower and don't get your cast wet, then get dressed or we will be late for dinner."

"Yes, dear."

Tom made his way to the shower as Jenny begin laying out clothes for both of them to wear for dinner."

Jenny placed his kit bag in the bathroom for him so as soon as he was out of the shower, he could shave and comb his hair.

Tom found it tricky taking his shower and get himself dried off while doing his best not to get his right arm and shoulder wet during the shower.

Tom was right-handed and doing everything with his left hand and arm was really hard for him.

After he finally dried off, he found he couldn't shave himself or comb his hair.

So, he asked Jenny to come and help him. She was able to help him and then said, "Tom, I have no idea how we are going to be able to get a shirt on you with your cast and your arm up against your chest."

"Jenny, the only thing I know is for me to put my left arm in the sleeve and pull the right side of the shirt as close as you can and have you button up the front of the shirt as high as you can.

"If we could find some type of clips with an elastic cord. We could hold the right side of the shirt as closed as possible and attach the other clip to the left side of the shirt. Do you have any idea of anything we could use to do that?"

"OK, Tommy let's get your shirt on your left arm and I'll do the best I can do to button the shirt up from the bottom of the shirt. Then I'll see what I can find to close the shirt up as much as possible."

Jenny pulled up his shirt and got his left arm in the sleeve and begin buttoning up the front of the shirt as high as she could.

Then Jenny said, "Let me think a bit and let me look through my bag to see what I can find to help hold your shirt closed."

Jenny opened her bag and found she had two large paper clips and a shoe bag that had a draw string.

She took the draw string out of the shoe bag and took one of the paperclips and worked it around and through the button hole, then she tied the string onto the first paper clip. Next, she put the second paper clip around the button and tied the string to it and pulled the shirt as tight as she could, then she tied it as tightly as she could.

Tommy looked in the mirror and said, "My darling, you are a very clever girl. You did it. I am proud of you."

"Tommy, I only hope it will stay tied through dinner. I don't want you popping out of your shirt during dinner."

"Yes, dear, now can you get my pants on and my socks and shoes?"

"OK, but I can see I am going to have to get you a man to help dress, or I'll never be ready for dinner on time again."

Jenny helped pull on and pull up Tom's pants and Tom found he couldn't even fasten his pants or his belt.

"Jenny, I have been hurt many times before, but I never had a problem of not being able to use my right arm to dress myself. I am as helpless as a baby."

"It's OK, Tommy. I'll help you and I am sure you will be feeling better before too long and maybe you can learn you can use your left hand more."

"I certainly hope so."

"Don't worry, you will. Now that you are ready, please sit down and give me a chance to get dressed for dinner."

"OK, my love. I'll sit myself down and you get yourself ready."

Tom sat down on one of the very plush chairs to wait for Jenny to get ready.

It seemed like only a short time later and Jenny announced, "OK, Tommy, I'm ready to go to dinner."

"I think that has to be the shortest wait I have ever had waiting for you to get ready."

Jenny just smiled and said, "Can you use your left hand to push the button for our maid to come to take us for dinner?"

Tom pushed the call button and in only a few seconds they heard a soft knock on their door.

Tom said loudly, "Come in."

The door opened and their maid came into their suite and asked, "You ready for dinner?"

Tom replied, "Yes, we are."

The maid said, "Please follow me to dining room.

Tom and Jenny got up from their chairs and Jenny took hold of Tom's left arm and the two of them began to follow their maid.

It took about five or six minutes walking before they came to a large dining room, which Tom thought could seat maybe as many as twenty-four people for dinner.

Tom thought the room was very well decorated and furnished like some of the English castles he had seen for the queen.

Omar greeted them and asked, "Was there anything you needed in your rooms?"

Jenny replied, "No, I think you have everything that we might need for our stay in our rooms. You seemed to have thought about everything your guests might need. Thank you."

"Good, I am pleased we are looking out for you as we should. So, how are you feeling, Tom?"

"Pretty weak and I am sorry to say. I had never realized how hard it is to do things like getting dressed with only one hand.

"My God, I found I couldn't put on my pants by myself. I had to have Jenny dress me to get here for dinner. Unbelievable."

"Don't feel too bad, Tom. I am certain that in a few days you will be able to do a lot more things for yourself."

"I certainly hope so, Omar. Right now I feel like a big baby. I am not even sure I can feed myself using my left hand. I never considered what people who had lost an arm had to go through to take care of themselves.

"I hope I don't have to find out what it's like to go through life with just one arm or like some people who were born with no arms."

Omar asked, "Tom, what has the doctor said about you getting back the function in your right arm?"

"Actually, I don't know that he has said much about it or if I would totally recover the use of my arm or not, do you know, Jenny?"

"No, all I know is that he expects you to have full recovery of your shoulder and arm."

Omar said, "Tom, then I think you should stop worrying about it. Sounds like you will be without the full use of your right arm for only a short time."

"Thank you, hope you're right, Omar. I'm sure that Jenny can take care of me until I get my right arm working like it should be. Isn't that right, Jenny?"

"My love, I will take care of you even if your arm never gets back to working the way it did.

"However, Omar is right, you will soon recover the full use of your arm."

The maid pulled out a chair next to Omar for Jenny, seating her on Omar's left side and a chair for Tom on Omar's right side.

Both of them took their seats and Omar said, "Jenny, you look lovely this evening and it is certainly nice to have the opportunity to meet you and to see my friend Tom again.

Tom said, "Omar, we really want to thank you for agreeing to take us in and to keep us safe while I am recovering from my wound."

"Tom, you are my friend and I want you to know how much I appreciate all of the things you did to help me and my country.

"Without meeting you and General Hayes, my life would have never been what it is now.

"It is so much better for me and my people now. I was able to learn so much and how to look after my people.

"They all have a much better life now. The money I received from America changed everything for all of us.

"We are happier, healthier and better educated. We now have something to look forward to help make our country better now and in the future."

Tom replied, "Omar, that's one of the nicest things I've heard in a long time. Hearing we made life better for you and your people."

"Don't get me wrong, Tom, my poor country has a long ways to go, but at least our small area of our country is doing very well.

"Thanks for the opportunity to have enough money to learn we don't have to live the same old way that we've lived for many years.

"Really, we all lived just hand to mouth and most people lived with no hope for a better life and a peaceful future."

As Omar finished his speech the maid began bringing in their dinner plates and Tom was pleased to find the portions were reasonable and the food was very well prepared.

Their meal was excellent and Tom was able to feed himself with his left hand, awkwardly, but he managed to get through the whole meal.

Tom said, "Omar, tell me about Colonel John Strong, How did you find him to help you with the defense of your territory?"

"Tom, actually I didn't find him. Your people with the CIA put him in touch with me and suggested I consider hiring him to help protect my territory and my people from the Taliban.

"I've learned a lot from John. He's helped me to establish a perimeter around our entire area. Something like what he helped to set up for the defense of the Suez's Canal."

"Omar, after I have some time to heal a bit, I would love to take a tour of what you have done on the perimeter of your territory."

"Tom, I would like to show you what we have established and see what you think about our work.

"Also, I want you to get acquainted with John and see if you are as impressed as much with him as I am."

"I'd love to have the chance to spend time with John and talk about all of the things that have been accomplished in your area for you and your people's safety."

"Tom, I believe you will find you and John have a lot in common with your history in the military.

"Omar, I have to compliment you of your new grasp of English, it excellent."

"Again, it's due to John's influence and me hiring an English teacher from America. She works with me and my key staff members daily, helping us to speak better English.

"As John says, if you want to get along in this world it's necessary to be able to converse in English.

"It's also helped by teaching my senior officers English. Since the Taliban leaders have very little knowledge of English. So even if they could get our radio transmissions, they can't understand what we are saying."

Jenny said, "Omar, I know Tom would love to spend all night talking with you about all the changes you have made since we first met you, but he needs to take his meds and get some rest."

"Of course, Jenny. I understand. Is there anything we could do to help you with Tom?"

"No, thank you, Omar. I think I need to get him to bed so he has time to get some rest to help heal his wounds."

Omar pushed a button under the dining table and the maid who brought them to the dining room quickly came to take them back to their quarters.

Tom said, "Thank you, Omar, for a wonderful dinner and all that you are doing for us. I do hope one day we can pay you back for all the things you are doing."

"It's nothing compared to what you and America have done for me and my people."

The maid quickly took them back to their quarters and asked if there was anything she could do to help them.

Jenny replied, "No thank you. We will be OK and we will see you in the morning."

The maid replied, "Good night and if need anything push button and I will come."

Then the maid left and Jenny began helping Tom get undressed and into bed. She found it much easier taking Tom's clothes off than helping him get dressed.

They were both soon in bed and fast asleep.

8

om woke up the next morning feeling much better and found that Jenny was already up and dressed. Jenny asked, "Are you feeling better this morning?" "Much better. I certainly got a good night's sleep and I'm sure not hurting as much as I had been all day yesterday."

"Good, maybe you are beginning to heal that shoulder and arm up."

Tom replied, "I don't think there was anything wrong with my shoulder, just the arm, but having my arm pulled up against my chest is causing my shoulder to hurt too."

"I know the doctor didn't want your arm moving around much so he decided to pull it up to your chest, so you couldn't be moving your arm all around."

"Well I don't care what the doctor thinks. I think I would feel better if I just had my arm in a sling. I think we should try to contact the doctor and see if he would agree to let my arm just rest in a sling."

"OK, Tom, we can call him today and ask him if we can take the bandages off that are holding your arm against your chest. OK?"

"Great, I know I would do better if my arm wasn't up against my chest. It's awful. I can't get dressed or feel like myself like this."

"Right now, Tom, how about I help you get cleaned up and dressed and have some coffee and breakfast"

"OK my love, help me get washed up, shaved, brush my teeth and comb my hair."

After Jenny had spent about thirty minutes helping Tom do all of these things it was time to get him dressed.

She said, "Tom, you know you are a lot harder to take care of than Tommy, because you're so much bigger and I don't have to help him shave like I do for you.

"Sorry my love. I hope you won't have to keep helping me for too much longer.

"I certainly want to get back to being able to take care of myself. I don't like needing someone to take care of me."

"I'm sure you don't, so from now on don't let the bad guys hurt you."

"Jenny, that's the best advice anyone has given me for a long time."

Both of them started laughing at Tom's statement.

Jenny retorted, "Well, it's the truth."

Then she said, "OK, let's get you dressed so we can have breakfast."

Tom had a short sleeve military undershirt that Jenny could get over his head and then get his left arm through the sleeve and then just let the undershirt hang down over his right arm and chest.

Then she found an army fatigue shirt he had in his suitcase that she could get his left arm in and then put it over his right shoulder and arm.

She just let it hang down and kept it closed by using her large paper clips and string to secure the shirt.

Jenny picked up the phone and called their maid to let her know that they were ready for breakfast.

The maid asked what they would like for breakfast and Jenny told her that her husband would like ham, fried eggs, toast and coffee. Jenny said, she would like hard boiled eggs, toast, juice and plenty of coffee.

The maid told her she would bring their breakfast soon. About thirty minutes later the maid brought them their breakfast.

The maid said, "When breakfast finish. I take you both to General Omar's office. He wants you come there

After they finished their breakfast, Jenny called the maid to let her know they were ready to go see General Omar.

The maid said she would come soon. Only a few minutes passed before the maid was at the door. Jenny answered the door and the maid said, "Now, you come me and I take you to General Omar's office.

Tom and Jenny followed the maid and she took them to General Omar's office.

When they arrived there, his secretary told them, General Omar was having a meeting with Colonel Strong and their English teacher, Grace Adams, but he should be ready for them very soon.

Tom and Jenny sat down to wait for Omar and their maid left to go back to clean up their breakfast dishes and their room.

Suddenly, Omar opened his office door and asked Tom and Jenny to come in.

They followed Omar into his office and Omar said, "You have met Colonel Strong, but I would like you to meet our American English teacher, Miss Grace Adams."

Tom and Jenny saw this very nice looking young woman who was seated on the right side of Omar's desk.

Grace got up from her chair and walked up to Tom and Jenny and said, "I feel like I know both of you already.

"Having listened to Omar talk about you all the time. I do believe you two are his favorite people in the world.

Tom said, "I don't know anything about that, but he has a very special place in our hearts, after saving one of our closest friends."

Grace put her hand out to shake Tom's and Jenny's hands.

Tom took her hand and gently shook it and then released it so she could shake Jenny's hand.

Omar said, "Please have a seat." All three of them sat down around Omar's huge desk.

Then Omar said, "Tom, I want to take you and Jenny around to see what we have done to protect the perimeter of our territory and what we have done for our families."

Tom said, "Great, Omar, we would love to see what you have done for your people and how you are protecting your territory.

Omar said, "John, would you get a couple of our golf carts, so we can take Tom and Jenny to see what we have done for my people and how you designed the protection for our territory."

John replied, "Yes sir, I'll have two golf carts brought up to the castle's front doors." John got up and left the office to take care of the golf carts.

Omar continued talking telling Tom and Jenny about how lucky he was to have Grace Adams here to teach his men and him English.

Tom could see that Omar was just glowing when he talked about Grace and how much she had done by teaching him and his men English.

Tom thought to himself, Omar has a very strong feeling about Grace.

A few minutes later John came back in to let Omar know that they had the golf carts at the front doors of the castle.

Omar said, "Grace, unless you have something that you have to do right now. I would like to have you go with us and be with Jenny."

Grace replied, "No sir, I would be honored to go with her."

Omar directed them to the front doors of the castle where the golf carts were waiting for them.

When they arrived at the front doors of the castle. Omar said, "John, would you take Jenny and Grace in one of the carts and you can explain what you have designed to protect our territory from attacks?"

John replied, "Yes sir. I would be happy to escort the ladies and explain our protection system for your territory."

Omar said, "Thank you, John. I'll take Tom in the other cart and go over your plan with him."

So John got into one of the golf carts and Jenny and Grace joined him as Tom and Omar got into the other cart.

As they begin driving along Omar began to talk to Tom about a problem he had that he didn't have anyone one he could talk to about.

Tom said, "Omar, I would be glad to help you with your problem if I can.

Omar said, "My problem is something I couldn't talk about with John or any of my people."

"Tom said, "Omar, is the problem about someone like Grace?"

Tom, why would you say something like that?"

Well, I can see how you look at her and how you talk about her. Then what you said about all the things she has done for you and your men."

"OK, it's about Grace, I think I have fallen in love with her and I don't know what to do about it."

"Well, my friend, I'll tell you what you need to do, you need to tell her how you feel about her."

"But Tom, what if she doesn't even like me?"

"Then, you' ll just have to respect that she doesn't feel the same way about you."

"I don't know what she might do, she might just quit and go back to America and she's done so many good things for me and my people."

"Omar, what has she done for your people?"

"She made me learn to understand that each of my people deserve to have a decent place to live and that their life had value. Not only for themselves but for me as well."

"Omar, I think she has done a lot for you already. Just maybe she has feelings for you.

"One thing, you will never know unless you tell her how you feel and ask her how she feels about you.

"You have never been afraid of anything before in your life! You were even ready to take on the American Army if you had to when you had General Jack Hayes."

"Well, that was different. I was young and didn't know any better.

"I knew I had an American General and I wanted to get a lot of money to give him back to the Americans after I took him from al-Qaeda."

"Well, you also had some of the top al-Qaeda leaders that you kind of threw in on the deal."

Omar said, "Well, Tom, that was the best thing that ever happened for me and my people."

"Then, Omar, get you courage up and ask Grace how she feels about you."

"OK, Tom you're right. I'll do it today.

"Tom, we are getting close to our border and you will soon see how John designed our defense like he did for the Suez Canal.

"We have built two-story homes along the whole distances of my territory and gave the homes to families. They not only live in the homes, but the homes are all connected to an alarm system back to my castle, so we know if we have invaders in our territory.

"In between each home, about a half a kilometer away, we built guard houses on each side of each home."

"In addition, we do have some radar in some of our areas, but we can't cover the whole area.

"We hope we have picked the most likely areas that invaders would try to attack us.

"Then of course we have rivers on both sides of our territory, which also help protect us and only two bridges to watch."

Then they arrived at the home John had picked out to show off their security system.

John and the two women were just exiting the golf cart when Omar and Tom arrived.

John had told the people who lived in this home that he wanted to show some guests their home, so the people who lived there were ready to show the home.

Omar and Tom got out of the golf cart and begin following John and the ladies to the house.

Arriving at the door of the home, John knocked on the door and a lady met them and invited them in.

When all of the guests were in the house the lady who lived in the home told Omar that they were sorry they couldn't go upstairs to see the bedrooms, because one of her daughters was having a baby.

The lady told Omar her daughter's water broke a few minutes ago and another daughter was tending to her upstairs.

John said, "Thank you, we won't take much of your time. We'll just look around downstairs a few minutes.

"Please go back upstairs and help take care of your daughter and her new baby. We will go in just a few minutes."

The lady rushed upstairs to help her daughter deliver her new baby.

True to his word, John quickly showed them around downstairs and they left the house.

Jenny said, "Omar, you did a wonderful thing building your people such wonderful homes. You are to be congratulated for looking after your people like that. Are all of the houses you built like this one you showed us?"

"Yes, they are, most of our families have large families so I wanted them to have somewhere their whole family could live and would be proud of their home.

"I do have to give credit to Grace for the idea of building such homes, she inspired me to do it. In the past most all of my families lived in tents or lean-tos."

Grace said, "Well, I know Omar loved his people and he had the money to be able to do it, so I encouraged him to do it and he did."

Omar said, "Yes, she knew how to "encourage" me."

All of the other folks laughed at the way he said "encourage."

Omar added, "Well, some people are better at encouraging people than others, and Grace is the champion encourager."

Then the rest of the people really laughed at Omar's statement, but the loudest of all was from Grace.

When she stopped laughing. Grace said, "Omar, I didn't know I was that big of influence on you."

Tom said, "Well, Grace, I guess you know it now."

Omar just smiled and said nothing.

Then John said, "Omar, I need to get back to the castle to check on some of our communication equipment if that's OK?"

Omar replied, "Certainly, go ahead."

Tom said, "John, if it's all right with you. I think I need to go back with you because I think I need to lie down for a while."

Omar asked, "Tom, do you think you need to go back to the hospital?"

"No, I think I just need to take it easy for a while."

Jenny said, "I'll go back with you to be sure you are all right."

Omar said, "Grace, I guess you better ride along with me."

"OK, I will do that. I'm sure I need to try to influence you to do something, but right now I can't think of what it is.

Everyone laughed at Grace's statement.

Tom and Jenny got into John's golf cart and off they went back to the castle.

Omar got into his golf cart and Grace got in the cart with him.

As Omar and Grace were driving along, Omar suddenly pulled his golf cart over and stopped at a beautiful site overlooking the blue river flowing rapidly over some very large rocks.

Grace said, "This is such a beautiful spot. I don't think I have ever had the opportunity to see it before."

Omar said, "Yes, it is. Grace there is something I want to talk to you about."

"OK, Omar, what would you like to talk about? Have I done something wrong that I need to correct or do something better?"

Omar said, "No, Grace, you've not done anything wrong. I have a problem with you."

"Oh, Omar, I'm so sorry. I'll try to do better, if you just tell me what I done."

"Grace, you've done nothing wrong. I have fallen in love with you."

"Omar, are you sure?"

"I'm as sure as I can be since I've never been in love before, and I want to marry you."

"Oh, Omar, I've been in love with you from almost the first day we met, but I couldn't say anything because I'm just one of your employees."

Grace, will you marry me?

"Yes, I will marry you, but are you allowed to marry me. I'm a Christian and you are a Muslin."

"I don't know, I've never thought about getting married. I will have to ask Imam Xerxes. If not, I'll think about converting."

"Omar, be sure you want to marry me, you've been a Muslin all your life and I've been a Christian all of mine."

"Grace, we will work it out. I love you and I want to marry you.

"And I want to marry you, Omar."

Omar pulled Grace as close to him as he could and kissed her and she kissed him back.

After a very long kiss, Omar said, "We got to go, so I can talk with Imam Xerxes."

He gently released his hold on Grace and turned the golf cart around and away they went headed back to his castle.

9

Omar drove back to the castle and told Grace he would contact Imam Xerxes, so they could met with him about them getting married.

Omar called Imam Xerxes as soon as he got back to his office and left word with Imam Xerxes' assistant that he needed to see him as soon as he could.

In the meantime, Grace went back to her office and had an English class with some of her students.

It was one of the longest classes Grace ever had in her life, because all she could thinking about was marrying Omar. Even thought it was only forty-five minutes long and they were some of Grace's best students, it still was the longest one she ever had.

In the meantime, Imam Xerxes came to Omar's office and asked Omar what he could do for him?

Omar explained that he wanted to marry Grace, the American English teacher, and she was a Christian.

"Omar wants to know if a Muslim man could marry a Christian woman?

Imam Xerxes asked, "Omar, are you sure you want to marry this woman?"

"Yes, I'm very sure that I want to marry her. I love her as much as life itself."

The Imam said, "Well yes, our faith allows a Muslin man to marry a Christian woman because she believes in only one God, but she must agree to raise your children in the Muslim faith."

He added, "A Muslin woman is not allowed to marry a Christian man."

Omar asked, "What do we have to do to get married?"

The Imam explained, "You have to prepare a marriage contract, which I can help you with, and you must give her a Mahar, that's a Bridal Gift.

"Which is hers alone, even if you get divorced, she gets to keep the marriage gift.

"The other thing she should know is that she doesn't take your last name. Her name stays the same."

Omar asked, "When do we have a marriage ceremony?"

The Imam replied, "Well, some people have it later, but only after you both agree to the marriage contract and after you both sign it, and your two witnesses sign the contract, then you are married.

"You don't need a ceremony to be married, it's just a celebration of your marriage."

Omar said, "Thank you. I will talk with Grace, but I'm sure she will want a wedding ceremony."

The Imam said, "Most brides do."

Then Imam Xerxes left Omar's office and Omar left to find Grace.

Omar went to her office to find Grace as she was returning to her office after her finishing her class.

Omar saw her and said, "Well, I have had a meeting with Imam Xerxes and have all of the information on us getting married."

Grace asked, "So, can we get married?"

Omar replied, "Yes, I can marry a Christian woman, but you will have to agree to raise our children as Muslims."

Grace asked, "OK, what else do we have to do?"

The Imam said, "To get married, we have to prepare a marriage contract, which he said he could help us with.

"Then, we must both agree to the terms of the contract, we both have to sign the contract, have two witnesses to sign it and then we are married."

Grace asked, "What about the wedding ceremony?"

"The Imam told me that after we sign the marriage contract, we could have the ceremony any time to celebrate our marriage.

"Omar, you mean the marriage contract is the most important thing to show we are married."

"Yes, that's what he said. The Imam also told me that I must give you a Mahr, it means a Bridal Gift, which is yours alone and even if the marriage failed, you get to keep the gift.

"One other thing, the bride keeps her same name, she doesn't take the husband's last name."

Grace said, "These things are certainly different then what happens in America, but were not in America, are we?"

Then Grace said, "Do we have to get a marriage license in Afghanistan?""No, I never heard of such a thing as a marriage license, what is it?"

"It's a license you have to buy from the state where you are getting married."

"No Grace, we don't have anything like that here."

Grace said, "Well, since all we have to do is make a marriage contract, if you still want to marry me. I want to contact my parents and ask them to come for our wedding. Do you still want to marry me?"

Omar replied, "Yes, Grace, of course, I still want to marry you, or have you changed your mind?"

"No, I haven't changed my mind, I love you and want you for my husband."

Omar put his arms around Grace and gave her a big kiss and said, "I love you so much, contact your parents and ask them to come to our wedding.

"Please tell them to come as soon as they can. I can't wait to have you for my bride."

Omar took his arms from around Grace and said, "Contact your folks and ask them to please come to our wedding, but hurry."

Grace left to go back to her office and sent an email to her parents asking them to make arrangements to come to Afghanistan for her wedding.

She wanted them to know she was marrying her boss, Warlord Omar Hekmatyar.

When her mother got the email, she wasn't surprised at all. Both she and her husband had already known how Grace was feeling about this wonderful man, Omar, from all of her emails about him.

Her father, of course, knew all about Omar since he worked for the State Department.

Beth Adams, Grace's mother sent Grace this email: Dear Grace, I will talk with your father and ask him to make arrangements for us to come to Afghanistan for your wedding as soon as he comes home this evening. I will let you know as soon as I can what date we can arrive there. Love Mom

Three days later Grace received an answer to her email that read: "Darling Grace, We will be arriving in three weeks and we will be coming with Ambassador Mike Smith and his wife, Joan, who have been in Washington meeting with members of the State Department and the President.

"Do hope this is enough time for you to have all of your wedding plans made. Much love, Dad

Grace ran as quickly as she could to Omar's office and told his secretary she needed to speak to Omar.

His secretary said, "Grace, you can go on in, he's reading some report from Colonel Strong."

Grace knocked on his office door and heard him say, "Come in."

When Grace came into his office, Omar got up from his chair and said, "Hello, Grace, my love. What's going on?"

"I got an email from my father and he said he and my mother would be here in three weeks, isn't that great news?"

"Wonderful news, he didn't say what day they would be here, did he?"

"No, he said they were coming with the American Ambassador to Afghanistan, Tyler Smith and his wife, Joan."

"That's great news, we better get our marriage contract finished and signed before they get here."

"No, Omar, I want us to sign it as part of our wedding ceremony and then take our vows, OK?

"I don't think that would be any problem. I'll ask Imam Xerxes, if that's OK."

Omar picked up his phone and called Imam Xerxes, who answered his phone on the first rang.

Omar then asked him if there was a problem if they included the signing of the marriage contract as part of the wedding ceremony.

The Imam said, "No, it's not a problem, you can do it at the same time. You just have to sign the marriage contract first. "

Grace heard what he said and she said "Good, that's what I want."

Omar said, "OK, that's what we will do."

10

Tom had now been recovering for over four weeks and was doing much better. He still had his arm in a sling, but he thought, no he knew, he had full movement in his shoulder and his arm.

The doctor just wanted to give his shoulder a little more time to heal before he completely released him back to full duty.

However, Tom thought it was past time for him to get back on his assignment to find and kill al-Garde.

But, Jenny didn't think so, so he decided to cool it until after Omar and Grace's wedding.

After all, Omar had asked him to be his best man, so al-Garde would have to wait his turn.

But, Tom knew al-Garde would soon get his turn after killing several Americans soldiers and wounding him.

Al-Garde was on the top of Tom's list of thing he had to do and you never wanted to be at the top of Tom's list.

Two days later, two American Army helicopters arrived at the castle's heliport, bringing Grace's parents, Tyler and Beth Adams,

along with Ambassador Mike Smith and his wife, Joan for Omar and Grace's wedding.

In addition to those two couples, there were two more guests on those helicopters, General Jack Hayes and a new CIA Agent, Lt. Commander Serene Sessions.

There were two more helicopters in the sky, just to make sure that the two helicopters and their passengers were safe, during the landing and dropping off their passengers.

Grace and Omar were waiting just outside the castle's doors for their guests.

Tyler and Beth, along with General Jack Hayes were the first three passengers to come walking up to the castle doors.

Grace went hurrying out to meet her parents, and then they were soon having a three-person hug.

Omar had followed along behind her and when he saw General Jack Hayes, he rushed up to greet him.

Jack said, "Omar, is that you, you've lost so much weight and you look so much younger?"

Omar replied, "Well, it's the new and improved version of me. So how are you, my friend?"

"I'm doing great, I've just come along to help my old friend, Tom Parker, finish the mission, he came to Afghanistan to do."

About that time, Grace came up to Omar and Jack and said, "Omar, I want to introduce you to my folks, this is my dad, Tyler, and my mother, Grace."

Tyler put out his hand to Omar and Omar shook his hand and said, "Welcome to my home. I have been looking forward to meeting Grace's wonderful parents."

Tyler replied, "Well I don't know if we are wonderful, but we are her parents."

Omar answered, "I know you had to be wonderful parents in order to raise a wonderful, sweet daughter like Grace."

Beth then reached out to put her arms around Omar, but found Omar was so tall and big, she could only get her arms about half way around him.

Omar said, "I never even ever had my mommy put her arms around me when I was a little boy, but thank you it was so sweet of you to try."

Beth laughed and said, "Now I know why my daughter loves you so much, you are so sweet."

"Thank you mom, that's the nicest thing, anyone ever said to me."

Jack thought to himself, you should have met him when I first met him. No one would have thought Omar was sweet then, that's for sure.

No one would have believed what kind of person, Omar had become since meeting Jack and Tom and the other Americans. He had changed one hundred percent.

Jack introduced Ambassador Mike Smith and his wife, Joan, to Omar and Grace.

After the introduction Grace said, "I want to thank you for coming for our wedding. We are honored to have you join us for our happy occasion."

Ambassador Smith replied, "Thank you and Omar for allowing us to crash your wedding."

"No, Omar and I are honored that you could be with us for our wedding."

"Thank you, Grace, we feel the same way. I have known and respected your father for many years and when I was with him in Washington earlier this month, he told me about you getting married and I asked him if it would be all right if Joan and I came to your wedding."

"I'm so glad you and Mrs. Smith could come to our wedding."

Grace's father asked, "When will your wedding be."

"Tomorrow afternoon, we've just been waiting for you and mom to get here."

Jack asked, "Omar, how is my friend Tom Parker doing?"

"He doing a lot better now. I think he is about all healed up. He wasn't doing very well when he first got here."

Jack said, "Well, he's one tough son of gun. I'm so happy he is doing a lot better now. I was asked to come to see if I could help him finish his assignment."

Omar replied, "I'm sure he's about to go crazy sitting around here and not being able to finish his job and go home to be with his son."

"You know, Jack, he hasn't said anything to me about his son, how old is he now?"

"I believe he's about four or five."

About that time Tom and Jenny come out of the castle doors and Tom saw Omar was talking to his old friend, Jack Hayes.

Tom and Jenny headed directly toward Jack as quickly as they could to where Omar and Jack were standing.

When Jack saw them, he left Omar and came as fast as he could to meet them.

Tom said when they met together, "What are you doing here? You're supposed to be running the Pentagon."

"Well, my boss told me I had to come to take care of you before you got yourself and Jenny killed."

"Well, that was certainly nice of your boss to let you come here to save us. Normally, of course it's me that needs to come and save you."

"True, but this time he's afraid you've gotten too old and decrepit to finish this little job by yourself, so he sent me.

"What I really think is he's worried about Jenny and I told him, she was worth saving."

"Good, Jack, I'm glad you could take time away from your bridge games and golfing with the President to save us.

Jack said, "Well, the truth is I didn't want to miss Omar's wedding."

"So, Jack what do you think about the new Omar?"

"I think it's wonderful. I can't believe it's the same man that turned me over to the army, when he and his people saved me from al-Qaeda."

"Well, my friend, he is and what he has done for his people is unbelievable, it's like something out of a fairy tale."

Then Tom saw Commander Serene Sessions and shouted out to her, "Serene, what in the world are you doing here?"

Serene came up to where Tom, Jenny and Jack were standing and said, "Well, you told me to go with the CIA and I did, so they sent me here along with General Hayes to help you with your mission."

Tom said, "Serene, I'm glad somebody took my advice once, and I hope you enjoy being with the CIA. I know Jack needs all the help that he can get to save me."

Jack just smiled and said, "That's right, Serene, I certainly will need all the help I can get to keep this old guy alive."

Soon after that Omar had all of his new guests taken to their rooms and told them all to have a little rest. They would have dinner at eight and a staff member would come to their room and bring them to the dining room.

Omar's staff picked up the new guests' luggage and other staff members led them to rooms.

Promptly at eight p.m. a staff member knocked on their doors and brought all of the new guests to the large dining room, which Tom and Jenny hadn't seen before.

They could see it had been designed to hold a large number of people.

The tables had been sit up to just hold the told number of guests for the dinner that night, and again all of the furnishings were beautiful and well made, with comfortable seating.

There were nameplates for each guest. At the head of the table were: Omar and Grace: on Omar's right was Tyler, Beth, Tom, Jenny, and Jack; on the left side of the table next to Grace were Mike, Joan, Serene and Colonel John Strong.

The staff began to serve the first course as soon as all guests were seated. By anyone's standards the meal was superb and the service was equally impressive.

All of the diners enjoyed their dinner and everyone graciously thanked Omar for a wonderful meal and excellent service.

Omar and Grace simply smiled and thanked each guest and bade them good night and told them the wedding would be at two o'clock in the afternoon in the dining hall where they just had dinner.

Grace's parent's gave her and Omar each a hug and said they hoped they had a wonderful wedding tomorrow.

Tom, Jenny and Jack went back to Tom and Jenny's room to catch up on what was going on in all of their and their families' lives.

Ambassador Mike Smith and his wife, Joan, thanked Omar and Grace for a wonderful dinner and looked forward to attending their wedding.

Colonel Strong and Serene left to go to their own quarters and again thanked the happy couple for a wonderful dinner and said they were looking forward to the wedding.

11

Omar had asked Tom to be his best man at his wedding and Grace had asked Jenny to be her bridesmaid, so both of them would be part of their wedding.

Grace's father Tyler would escort Grace down the aisle. Everyone knew what part in the wedding they would play.

Tyler had brought his tuxedo with him to wear for the wedding, so he was all set.

Of course, Imam Xerxes would perform the wedding ceremony. Not that anyone at the wedding would have any idea of what was being said with Imam Xerxes officiating the wedding, since he had little or no English.

One of the ladies on the castle staff, Nan, was assigned to help take care of Grace and would be helping Grace and Jenny dress for the wedding.

Omar and Tom would have Omar's English dresser, Charles, helping them dress for the wedding.

Omar told Tom that Charles came to work for him because Colonel John Strong told him to be a real gentleman, he needed to have someone who would look after his wardrobe and help him dress properly at all times.

Tom thought Colonel Strong had a lot of influence on Omar. From Tom's viewpoint that was a good thing, considering how Omar was when Jack and he first met Omar.

By twelve-thirty Tom and Jenny were already in Omar's and Grace's bedrooms to be sure they would be ready for the two o'clock wedding.

Omar would be dressing in a brand new uniform that Charles helped design.

Tom thought when he saw it that it looked similar to a formal English Army dress uniform, although it was in a beautiful shade of green with a muted red stripe down the pant legs.

The jacket had gold colored buttons on the jacket, which was set off with the same red color of his tie. The jacket's sleeves had gold braid embroidered cuffs.

He would also be wearing the medal that Tom gave him when he freed Jack Hayes and brought high ranking al-Qeada prisoners to the US Army years ago.

Tom would also be wearing his dress American Army uniform with all of his medals, which covered the left side of his chest and had been earned over twenty-plus years of service and more battles than he wanted to talk about.

Grace would be wearing a beautiful white wedding dress with lace on the bodice; sleeves and the bottom hem. She also would be wearing a cathedral veil, which was a long flowing white train attached to a crown on her head that was set with pearls.

Jenny, would be dressed in a white evening grown, that she had made for her after she had been asked to be Grace's bridesmaid.

If you are a Billionaire and have your clothes made for you by a fashion designer in Hong Hong, you can get a custom-designed dress made for you in a few days and delivered to you anywhere in the world. It also helps if you wore the same dress size ever since you were twenty years old. Which Jenny did.

A few minutes before two o'clock, all of the bridal party made their way to two small rooms off of the dining hall.

Omar, Tom and Tyler, along with Charles, were in one of the rooms and Grace, Jenny and Nan were in the other room.

Exactly at two o'clock the wedding music began playing and Tom and Omar began their walk down the aisle and took their place on the right side of Imam Xerxes, who was standing directly behind a small table.

A few seconds after the men were in their place, Jenny started walking down the aisle until she reached where the men stood on the left side of the small table.

After Jenny was in her place, the wedding march began again and Tyler and Grace made their way down the aisle to where Grace's mother Beth was standing. Grace stopped and her mother gave her a hug and a kiss.

When the kiss was over, Tyler and Grace moved up next to where Omar was waiting and Tyler gave his daughter a kiss and returned to sit next to his wife.

At the same time, Grace stepped up next to Omar. Now all of the wedding party were in their places.

Then Imam Xerxes said, in Pushtu, "Omar and Grace, you both have read your marriage contract and agreed to the terms set forth on it.

"If so, you will both now sign the marriage contract."

Most of the guests at the wedding, who only spoke English, only understood the words "Omar and Grace" but had no idea what was going on with the wedding.

Omar took a pen and signed the contract and then Grace took the pen from Omar's hand and signed the document.

Then Imam Xerxes said in Pushtu, "Do you have the Mahr, the Bridal Gift?"

Omar replied in English, yes, my Bridal Gift is two million US dollars in gold coins.

Next, Imam Xerxes said in Pushtu, "Now we will move over to the Arch for the rest of the service."

All of the wedding party then moved over to what was now the center of the aisle and the wedding party stood in front of a beautiful flower- decorated Arch.

After the wedding party was all in their places, Imam Xerxes began in broken English a traditional wedding ceremony and he asked, "Omar, take the woman for wife?"

Omar replied, "Yes, I take Grace for my wife."

Then the Imam asked, "Grace, take Omar for husband?" Grace replied, "Yes, I take Omar for my husband." The Imam said, "Now you husband, kiss bride." Omar didn't hesitate, he put his arms around Grace and placed a big kiss on her lips.

Then they started back down the aisle headed to an area on the other side of the large hall.

After they passed by the pew in which Ambassador Mike Smith and his wife Joan were sitting, Joan leaned over and asked her husband, "What's with this Bridal Gift, what's that all about?"

Mike said, "The Muslim traditional wedding requires the groom to give his wife a so called Bridal Gift, which is hers alone. He has no claim on it even if they divorce, she keeps the Bridal Gift, in other words he has no claim on her gift."

Joan asked, "Did he say her gift was two million US Dollars in gold coins?"

"Yes, that's what I understood."

Mike said, "It was a good thing we weren't Muslin when we got married in college, your Bridal Gift would have been a couple of candy bars.

Then Joan said, "Next time, I get married., I'm marrying a rich Muslim man."

Mike said, "Good luck."

Just as everyone was beginning to move over to the reception area of the hall, they heard a huge explosion outside."

Omar yelled, "Colonel Strong, quick, get my wife and all of our guests down to the safe room and stay with them until we know everything is all right."

Then Omar said, "Tom, Jack, Jenny and Serene, come with me."

Quickly the five of them headed to the front door of the castle. On their way one of Omar's men was passing out automatic weapons and belts of ammunition for the weapons, He gave all of them a weapon and two belts of ammo.

Omar led the group to the front door of the castle, there he had Jack help him move some special iron barriers across from the entrance to the front doors of the castle.

The castle doors were specially made reinforced iron doors which should preclude anyone from breaking the doors down.

However, Omar knew that enough explosive would sooner or later blow the doors away.

They could hear lots of firing and people getting closer to their doors.

They could also hear people screaming in pain from getting hit with bullets.

Then, suddenly they heard lots of firing from machine guns and the sound of helicopters.

Then they could only hear the sound of the helicopters' engines. The firing of weapons was gone.

The next thing they heard was knocking on the front doors and then it stopped, then after silence for time enough to count to twenty-five, the knocking begin again.

That's my men, that's the signal that it's OK to open the castle doors.

Omar and Jack moved the barriers away and opened the doors.

Omar asked, "How bad was it?"

One of his men said, "We lost seven men and have ten more men injured.

"They were getting close to breeching the castle doors, but two of America's helicopters came and killed all of the men closest to the doors. Then the rest of them fled into the jungle.

Omar said, "Thank you and please give me a report of the name of the men killed and wounded as soon as you can.

Then Omar said, "Let's get the folks out of the safe room."

A few minutes later, they opened the door to the safe room and everyone was happy that the attack was over and that everyone in the castle was OK.

Omar said, "Please, everyone, come upstairs, since we have a wedding cake to cut and ice cream to eat."

12

everal minutes passed and they heard the helicopters coming back and landing on the heliport, behind the castle.

Omar asked Colonel Strong if he would go out and check on the people in the helicopters and if they were OK to please invite them in to have some wedding cake and ice cream.

A few minutes passed before Colonel Strong returned with the two crews from the helicopters and they told Omar they appreciated the opportunity to have a piece of his wedding cake and ice cream.

While Omar and Grace were thanking the men for fighting off the men attacking their home, Ambassador Smith heard Omar tell them if it hadn't been for them and their helicopters, he was afraid the invaders would have breached the castle.

Hearing that, Ambassador Smith said, "Omar, I think considering what you and your men have been doing helping us in our mutual cause in Afghanistan, I believe

you should have a couple of helicopters to help you defend your territory."

Omar replied, "That would be wonderful, but we wouldn't have anyone that would know how to fly them."

The Captain of the helicopters said, "Well, I am sorry, but we don't have any extra pilots that could spend the time teaching your people to fly them. Every one of our pilots are pulling double duty all ready."

Tom was listening to this whole conversation and said, "Omar, you have one of the best helicopter pilots that I've ever flown with here already."

Omar said, "Tom, I have no idea who that could be."

Tom replied, "Lt. Commander Serene Sessions, she's a great pilot. She pulled me and my family out of the Bering Sea not long ago."

Serene spoke up and said, "I'm not sure that I'm a great helicopter pilot, but I would be happy to teach several of your men to fly them."

Tom said, "Trust me, she's a great pilot. I've flown with a lot of helicopter pilots so I know how good she is."

Ambassador Smith said, "I guess that solves that problem, so I'll see what I can do about get you two helicopters, Omar."

Omar said, "Thank you, Ambassador Smith, that would be greatly appreciated."

It was now almost five o'clock in the afternoon and Omar said, "If everyone has had their fill of cake and ice cream, I would like to suggest we all take a few hours break before we have dinner at eight here in the dining hall.

"If you helicopter crews can stay, we would love to have you as our honored guests."

The Captain in charge said, "Thank you Omar, but we need to get back to our base. We want to thank you for the invitation but we really can't stay any longer."

Omar said, "We are the ones thanking you for coming to our aid. Bless all of you."

The crew's Captain smiled and said, "Thank you and congratulations on yours and Grace's wedding. We were honored to be of service to you both."

After saying that, the two helicopter crews got into their helicopters and were soon on their way back to their base.

Omar and Grace made their way up to their new quarters after their wedding.

Grace had asked Omar if she could decorate the new large suite of rooms that would be their bedroom and bathrooms after they were married and, of course, he agreed to let her do it.

Omar had not seen what their new bedroom suite looked like, but he knew if Grace did it, there was no question that he would love it.

The two of them made their way to their new bedroom and when they arrived there.

Grace opened the doors of their bedroom suite and asked Omar to come and see what she had made for them.

Omar first saw a sitting room with large comfortable looking stuffed chairs and couches. The room even had a very large desk and chair for him to work at.

Omar said, "I love it, what else have you done?"

Next, Grace took his hand and led him into their bedroom.

When they got there, Omar was shocked to see the largest bed he had ever seen in his life.

Grace had it specially made for them, it was eight feet wide and ten feet long.

Omar couldn't believe it, he had to lie down on it right now.

He just had to try it to see if he could lie down on it and stretch his legs out and not have his legs and feet hanging over the end of the bed.

Omar said, "Grace, it's wonderful, where did you get such a big bed."

"I had it made for you, along with the sheets, pillow cases, blankets and bed spread."

Omar got off of the bed and took Grace in his arms and said, "I love you so much and thank you for having a special bed made for us."

After they hugged and kissed for a long time, Grace said, "You have to see what else I have done."

Then she led him into a large dressing room, with huge closets on each side of the room. One for Omar and one for her.

During their wedding, the staff moved all of their clothing into their new quarters, along with everything from their bathrooms and had everything put away.

Off of their dressing room were two large bathrooms. complete with sinks, toilets, bidets, bathtubs and showers.

Omar's counter top and sink were extra high to accommodate his height so he didn't have to lean so far over to use it.

Again, everything in his bathroom was specially made in a larger size for his six foot seven frame.

Omar said, "Oh Grace, thank you for doing all of this for me. I had no idea that you could have special things made like that for people like me, who are just too big for everything."

Grace replied, "You're not too big, you're just right for me, my love."

Again, Omar took her in his arms and began kissing her and told her she was everything he ever wanted.

They talked about changing clothes but decided they shouldn't since they didn't tell their guests they were planning to.

So they continued to stay in the clothes they worn for the wedding: she in her wedding gown and he in his specially-made uniform.

It was now close to the time they needed to go back down to the dining hall where everything had now been put back as a dining room for their wedding dinner.

Omar thought his staff had done a wonderful job taking care of moving all of his and Grace's things to the new bedroom suite and changing the dining room back after using it as their wedding chapel.

The wedding dinner was excellent, everything went well for their wedding day, except for having the raiders attacking the castle and killing and wounding several of his men.

'Omar was sure that no one at his and Grace's wedding had ever encountered a wedding day like theirs.

Dinner was wonderful and everyone certainly enjoyed it and the visiting after dinner, but by nine-thirty, Omar and Grace had slipped away for their wedding night. They would enjoy that, too.

13

The next morning Tom told Jenny, it's time for us to complete our mission. You know, the one we came here to do, kill al-Garde, so we can go home.

Jenny asked, "How can we do that, we have no idea where he is."

"We may not know actually were he is, but you can be sure, he's not very far from this castle this morning."

"Tom, why would you say that?"

"What happened here yesterday?"

"The castle was attacked, that's what happened.

"My darling Jenny, why do you think it was attacked, he knows we're here. Somehow, he found out that I am here, and he swears he is going to kill me. No matter what it takes to accomplish that.

"Except, my darling, we are going to kill him, before he has another chance to kill me."

Jenny said, "So, OK, exactly how are we going to do that my darling husband?"

"OK, right now. I don't have any idea on how we are going to do it, but we are."

Jenny replied, "Then, let's get dressed and have some breakfast and like Scarlet O'Hara said, "We'll think about that tomorrow."

"OK, Scarlet, I'll think about it tomorrow and today and we'll get Jack involved in helping us think about it."

"Well, Captain Rhett Butler, you better do a good job of thinking about it or General Sherman might just get you.

So they both got dressed, but now that Tom was healed up enough, he could dress himself.

Of course, he was dressed and ready to go long before Jenny was ready.

Tom thought, OK things are almost back to normal now in my life, I'm waiting for Jenny.

When they arrived in the dining room the first person they saw was his old friend, Jack Hayes.

Jack looked up from his plate and said, "Good morning, you two, how are you doing this morning?"

Tom replied, "We're doing just fine. After breakfast, I would like for you to come to our room and help us figure out how we're going to get al-Garde."

Jack said, "Sounds like a good plan to me, let's get him so we can get back to our real life.

"I'm sure Beverly Hills is missing you two and the Pentagon is certainly missing me, but my wife is missing me more. She wants me to come home before you get us all killed."

Tom replied, "One thing for sure, Beverly Hills is missing Jenny. Their economy is down five points since she's been gone."

Jenny said, "I told my daughter to be sure to spend a lot while I was gone. I guess she is letting me down."

Jack replied, "I'm sure glad we don't live there, my wife would be so mad that she couldn't keep up with Jenny's spending."

Tom answered, "No, one can."

Then Jenny cooled her husband and their friend with just a look, "I've never spent more money than I have."

Tom agreed, "You're right about that. You would have to hire a bunch of people to help you, yes sir, a really big bunch of people."

Jenny and Jack just laughed at Tom statement.

Tom said, "OK, let's have some breakfast and then we can figure out how we are going to get al-Garde."

A few minutes later all of the rest of the wedding guests joined them for breakfast.

After they finished their breakfast there was still no sign of the newlyweds.

Someone said, "I wonder if we'll see Omar and Grace today?"

About that time Colonel John Strong came by and said, "I've talked to Omar and he asked me to tell everyone that they wouldn't be coming down for breakfast, but thought they would see everyone at lunch."

Everyone just smiled and said nothing.

Tom thought to himself, maybe they would and maybe they won't. He could understand that.

After breakfast was over, the three of them went directly to Tom and Jenny's suite.

The three of them sat down in the living room. Tom begin to talk about what they needed to do to get al-Garde.

He said, "The only thing we know about al-Garde now is that I am very sure al-Garde had found out, somehow, that he and Jenny were staying at Omar's castle.

"Which meant it was likely that al-Garde was not far from where they were right now.

"But that was still a problem, because it's a virtual jungle across the river from the castle. You know it's almost impossible to find someone in there."

Jenny said, "It sounds like we would have to find a way to draw him out if we were going to be able to have any chance of killing him."

Jack added, "I think we would have to set you two up as targets to have any chance of getting him to show his face."

Jenny replied, "Wow, I don't think that's a very good idea, he almost killed Tom the last time."

Tom said, "Maybe we could set up something that looked like us in a vehicle leaving the castle and then when he tried to get us, we could get him."

Jack asked, "Just how would you do that?"

Tom responded, "Well, right now I have no idea how we could do that, but let me think about that for a minute."

The three of them started drinking the coffee that Jenny had made while Tom and Jack were talking.

Tom said, "I have an idea of how we might be able to set up such a plan to get al-Garde to show himself.

"We know he's got people watching the castle. So what if we have the CIA bring back the vehicle they used to bring us here, to take us back to Kabul?"

Jack asked, "How is that going to keep you safe and let you have a chance to get al-Garde."

Jenny said, "Jack, one thing you don't know is that this vehicle is almost completely safe, with its armor-plated body and special bullet-proof glass and an armor-plated undercarriage.

"It's built like a tank, but it's a specially built extra-large Land Rover. It's so big, it has to have four rear tries to hold its weight, some rich planter had it specially made for him."

Jack said, "OK, Jenny. I can understand how you two can be safely taken out of here in that vehicle, but how do you get al-Garde?"

Tom answered, "Jack, what we do is start driving through this jungle and about halfway out of the jungle, the vehicle quits running and we become a sitting duck.

"I'm pretty sure that al-Garde wouldn't miss an opportunity to come after me like that.

"We just continue sitting there waiting on someone to come looking for us and that would give al-Garde and his men a chance to attack the vehicle."

Jack said, "OK, you're sitting ducks. So what happens when al-Garde and his men attack the vehicle."

Tom says, "The two helicopters that have been sitting behind the castle suddenly come swooping down and kills all of the attackers, including al-Garde. Mission finished."

Jack said, "Well it could work, but you could also do some coordination and drop some troops behind his men to make sure that none of them can get away."

Tom said, "Now, your sounding like a general."

Jack said, "By damn, Tom. I am a general, don't you know that, colonel?"

Tom snapped back, "Yes, sir. General Hayes."

Then the three of them beginning laughing.

Then Tom said, "We need to find out if Ambassador Smith is going to have any luck getting those two helicopters for Omar."

Jack said, "Yeah, that plan sure is not going to work without having the helicopters."

Tom replied, "No Jack, without the helicopters we would really be sitting ducks, because no matter how strong that vehicle is with enough explosives. They would finally blow off the doors or something."

Tom said, "I'm going to try to call Ambassador Smith to see if he has had time to check on the helicopters."

Tom took his cell phone out of his phone holster and placed a call to the Ambassador.

A few minutes later Ambassador Smith answered and said, "Hello, Tom, what can I do for you today?"

"Mr. Ambassador, I was wondering if you had time to check to see if there was any hope of getting Omar those two helicopters."

"I'm glad you called Tom. I contacted the Pentagon and asked about getting those helicopters for Omar.

"Here's what they told me: that since the President is talking about pulling all of our troops out of Afghanistan that would be two less things they would have to move out of the country.

"So they said they would make arrangements to get two helicopters delivered to Omar this week, plus a lot of spare parts to be sure he could keep them flying."

Tom asked, "Ambassador, what do you think of the decision to pull all of our troops out of Afghanistan?"

"Just between me and you and not for publication, I think it's a bad decision, but I don't make those kind of decisions.

"Frankly, by us leaving the country, it's just giving the radicals total control over the country."

Tom replied, "That's too bad, there's a lot of very good people living here."

"Yes, I agree, but this has been the longest war our country has ever been in and we have too many people pushing the President to get our troops out of here.

"So we're leaving the people that we've been here to protect by themselves, it's going to be a bloody mess.

"One other thing, by our leaving here, we'll be losing the ability to quickly strike a lot of other potential hot spots in this part of the world.

"There are a lot of enemies of America in this part of the world that will be cheering our exit from Afghanistan for that reason."

Tom replied, "Well, I'm really sorry to hear that, but I guess you've done all you can do to try to change the President's mind."

"Thank you, Tom. Believe me, I've tried everything I can think of, but the President has a lot more people pushing him to get our troops out of Afghanistan.

"Not only the opposition party, but leaders of his own party are now tired of hearing about some of our military people being killed or wounded here.

"No one can see the problems being resolved in this country by us, including myself."

Tom said, "Ambassador Smith, thank you for letting me know that Omar will get his helicopters and we'll have Commander Sessions training several of Omar's men to fly them.

"Thank you, Tom. I hope you can finish your assignment and that you and your wife can go home to Beverly Hills very soon."

Tom hung up the phone and said to Jack, "Omar going to get his helicopters, and from the way the Ambassador talked, he should get them this week."

Jack asked, "What was all of the rest of that long conversation about, Tom?"

"The ambassador was telling me that our military will soon be pulling out of Afghanistan.

Jack said, "Well, at the Pentagon our people have been working on the plans to pull all of our troops and equipment out of Afghanistan for several weeks now.

"So, I guess the President has finally made a decision to do it.

"Frankly, I know he is personally against, it but he can only fight so many battles at a time and Congress is pushing him to get us completely out of Afghanistan. So I guess that's the end of it here for us."

Tom said, "Well, except for a personal reason, I suppose we could just pack our baggage and go home. But I'll be damned if I do it until I get al-Garde. That will be one less thing the Afghans will have to worry about."

Jenny, who had just been listening to all of this, finally said, "Tom, you need to tell Omar that he's getting the helicopters and the plan you two have come up with to get al-Garde."

Tom replied, "Yes, Jenny, you're right. We are going to need his men helping us to pull this off."

Jenny said, "OK, let's go see Omar and get this show on the road."

14

Tom, Jenny and Jack went to Omar's office and found out he hadn't come into the office yet. His secretary said that he called and said he would be down in about thirty minutes.

She suggested they should just wait in his office, because he should be there in just a few minutes.

Tom asked if she could get Commander Sessions on the phone so he could talk with her.

She said she could. She called and Serene answered right away.

The secretary asked her to please hold for a call from Tom Parker, he needed to speak to her.

The secretary handed the phone to Tom and he asked Serene to come down to Omar's office, because she needed to be in a conversation they would be having with Omar and they would be waiting for her in his office.

She told him she would be right there.

Then Tom said to the secretary, "Thank you, we well just wait in Omar's office, as you suggested.

The three of them went in to Omar's office and sat down around his conference table.

They had only been waiting for a few minutes before Serene arrived to join them in Omar's office.

Only a few minutes more passed before Omar and Grace came into his office, holding hands and smiling at each other.

They were surprised to see the four of them sitting around Omar's conference table.

Omar said, "Good morning, how are you four doing this fine morning?"

Tom smiled and replied, "Not as well as you two."

Omar just kept smiling and said, "Yes, we are doing very well, thank you."

Tom said, "We just wanted you to know that you are going to get your helicopters."

"That's great news, do you know when they will be coming?"

"Ambassador Smith said they would be here this week."

"That's great, he didn't say what day they would be coming, did he?"

"No, Omar he didn't, but I have some other news that you are not going to be happy about."

What's that Tom?"

The US is pulling all of their troops out of Afghanistan " very soon.

"You're, right Tom. That's not good news. For the sake of my country, that's very bad news. Do you know when they're leaving?"

"The only thing we know is, it's going to be right away; that's one of the reasons they are so willing to give you the two helicopters and a lot of spare parts, so you would be able to keep them flying."

"Well, Tom, do you have any more great news like that?"

"No, Omar, but we do have a plan to get al-Garde and his men if you are willing to help us."

"OK, Tom, what do you need for us to do?"

While this conversation was going on, the rest of the people in the room remained quiet.

Omar and Grace continued standing and holding hands and Jenny, Jack, and Serene, just watched Omar's and Tom's facial expressions.

Tom said, "Omar, why don't you and Grace sit down at your conference table and we will explain our plan."

So Omar and Grace took seats at the conference table and Tom said, "I'm going to let Jack and Jenny lay out our plan."

Omar said, "Before you tell me your plan, I want to get Colonel Strong here so he can hear it, too."

Tom replied, "No problem, we will just wait until he gets here."

About that time Omar heard his secretary say good morning to Colonel Strong."

Before the colonel could answer her, Omar opened his office door wider and said, "John, please come into my office."

Colonel Strong immediately came into Omar's office and saw all the people sitting at Omar's conference table and said, "Good morning, everyone."

Omar said, "Colonel, would you please join us to hear a plan they have for getting those people who attacked the castle yesterday."

Colonel Strong found a chair and sat down to hear this plan.

Tom said, "Colonel, we were just about to present a plan we devised to get al-Garde and his men. We are sure he and his men are the ones who attacked the castle yesterday.

"I going to turn this meeting over Jack and Jenny now."

Jenny said, "Omar, do you and Colonel Strong, remember the Land Rover that the CIA used to bring Tom and me here after we were attacked in the Army Hospital in Kabul?"

Omar said, "I do, I remember it was a very different looking Land Rover, because it had four rear wheels. Never saw any Land Rover that looked like that before."

Colonel Strong shook his head, yes, to indicate he remembered the vehicle.

Jenny replied, "Yes, that's right. It had to have those extra rear wheels because the vehicle weighed so much since it had so much armor plating.

"It was built like a tank. Anyway, Tom's idea was to have the CIA bring that vehicle back to take us to Kabul."

Omar asked, "So how does that help you to get al-Garde?"

Jack replied, "Well, Tom believes that al-Garde is still watching your castle and is planning to try again to get him and Jenny.

"If that's right, then his people would be watching any vehicle traveling through the jungle that's across from you territory.

"Tom's idea is that he and Jenny would be in the special Land Rover and about half-way through the jungle they would stop the vehicle to look like it broke down."

"Al-Garde's people would see the vehicle just sitting there and Tom thinks al-Garde would attack the vehicle and when they did, your two helicopters would come in and kill him and most of his men.

"I suggested to Tom, that your men should be backing up the helicopters from both sides of where the vehicle stopped and then your people could get anyone trying to get away after the helicopters begin their attack."

Omar said, "Well, I believe that would work, if al- Garde was still waiting in the jungle on the other side of the river to try to kill Tom and Jenny."

Tom asked, "Omar, would you be willing to risk your men to try to be sure we get al-Garde and all his men?"

"Yes, if the helicopters are really going to be here.

Tom said, "I'm sure they are going to be here, because my friend, Three Star General, Jack Hayes, is going to call up the commander of the Army Forces in Afghanistan and order him to have them here.

"Since, Commander Sessions wouldn't have had enough time to train new pilots that we need for the attack, we would have to have the helicopters pilots stay with us until we can make that attack."

Then Tom turned to Jack and said, "That's right, isn't it, General?"

"Yes, it is. I do need to get back to the Pentagon as soon as possible."

Omar then said, "It looks like you have a plan, Tom, so let's do it. What do you think, Colonel Strong?"

Colonel Strong replied, "Yes, Omar, it sounds like a good plan, although it sounds like Tom and Jenny and the driver would be the ones taking the biggest risk."

Tom said, "Well, we are willing to risk it and we will be depending on the rest of you to keep us safe."

Colonel Strong answered, "Then, I guess we have a plan to get al-Garde and his men."

Omar said, "All right, we can do our part. It's a go."

Tom then asked, "Omar, are you and Grace going to go on a honeymoon?"

Grace said, "You know, we haven't even talked about it."

Omar asked, "Do newly married couples normally go on honeymoons?'

Grace replied, "Yes, they do and I want to go on mine."

Jenny said, "Then Tom and I want to give you two your honeymoon trip. Have you ever been to Hong Kong?"

Omar replied, "No, I've read about it, but, no, I've never been there."

Grace said, "I've only changed planes there. So I would love to go to Hong Kong."

Jenny said, "When we finish our assignment. I'll have my plane pick us up in Kabul and take you two to Hong Kong.

"There you can stay in a suite in one of my buildings and have a car and driver available to take you all over the city and show you all around the city.

"Trust me, you will be completely taken care of on your honeymoon.

"When you are ready to go home, I'll have a plane bring you back to Kabul and then one of your helicopters can bring you on home."

Grace said, "That sounds wonderful, what do you think, Omar?"

"I think it sounds fantastic, but we can't let you do that, it's just too much."

Jenny replied, "It's nothing, compared to what you have been doing for us, you been keeping us alive and safe in your castle."

Tom said, "Forget it, Omar, you're going to lose, the wives have spoken. So you might as well learn it now, otherwise you're going to have a lot of miserable days and nights ahead of you."

Jack added, "Omar, listen, Tom knows what he talking about, learn it now and save yourself a lot of misery."

The women just laughed and then Jenny said, "See, your honeymoon is all set, just leave it to us girls and we'll take good care of you, like always."

Omar threw his hands up in the air and said, "Thank you, Jenny and Tom for a most wonderful honeymoon. I couldn't have planned it better myself."

Tom said, "I'm glad that's settled.

15

T om said, "Now, General Hayes, it's your turn to get on the telephone and gets us two helicopters and pilots.

Jack picked up his phone and checked his phone numbers and found a number for General Bob Johnson, commander of all troops in Afghanistan.

Jack pushed his number and when General Johnson answered he said, "General Hayes, how are things at the Pentagon?"

Jack replied, "Well I'm sorry to say I don't really know, because right now. I'm in Afghanistan with Warlord Omar." General Johnson said, "I'm sorry, sir. I didn't know you were in Afghanistan. What can I do for you?"

"I understand that we are giving Warlord Omar a couple of helicopters and a truck load of parts to help him to keep them flying."

"Yes sir, I understand that from Ambassador Smith's office. So what can I do to help you, General?"

"Bob, I know you've got your hands full, getting everything packed up and ready to ship everyone and all of our equipment back stateside.

"But I need a favor to help out a CIA assignment to capture or kill a fellow named al-Garde, but he's got quite an army and I need to get those two helicopters and two pilots for a few days at Omar's castle, so we can finish this assignment. It's one the President sent them on."

"OK, Jack, I'll contact the folks in charge of the helicopters and get them on their way to you this afternoon."

"Great Bob, I'll see to it that we get your two pilots back as soon as we finish this assignment."

"Jack, is there anything else I can do to help you while you're here?"

"No, I don't think so. I hope we can finish this and get out of here before you pull all of our troops out.

"Thanks again, Bob, for your help. We'll take good care of your pilots and get them safely back to you, I hope."

Jack turned to Tom and said, "Is there anything else I can do for you, Colonel Parker?"

"No sir, General Hayes. I think you have done your part.

Then Tom said, "I'll call Steve Troxler, you know the CIA agent in charge of the agents in Afghanistan, and ask him to have the special Land Rover brought here as quickly as he can."

So Tom called Steve and didn't get an answer. So, he left him a message to call back as soon as he could and let them know when he could have the special Land Rover brought back to Omar's castle.

About an hour later. Steve returned his call.

Steve said when Tom answered his phone, "So you're ready to go home now?"

"Not quite, we intent to finish our assignment before going home."

Steve asked, "So how are you going to do that?"

Tom went through every detail of his plan on the phone with Steve on how they were going to kill al-Garde.

After hearing Tom's plan, Steve said, "Well, it sounds like it could work if al-Garde is still hiding somewhere in that jungle."

Tom said, "Well, I'm pretty sure he and his men are still here and they are planning another attack on the castle to get Jenny and me."

Steve replied, "Maybe what he's really wants is to kill Omar to take over the castle and his people."

"You know Steve, I never thought about that, you may be right, he's looking for a twofer.

"Kill, me, Jenny and Omar and take over Omar's castle and he got his twofer and then he would have his people and the territory."

Steve said, "You know he's needs a new home for himself and his people and there isn't anywhere in the country, that's in better condition than Omar's."

"Well, Steve, you might be right. I'm telling Omar your idea and that should give him and his men plenty of incentive to really put out on an all-out effort to get al- Garde and all of his men."

Steve replied, "If that won't do it, nothing will."

"OK, Steve, back to my question. When can you have the Land Rover here?"

"Will tomorrow do?"

"That would be great, but can you have your people who are bringing the vehicle stay a day or two?"

"Yes, they'll stay as long as you need them."

"Great, thank you. One more thing, what's going to happen to your operations, now that the army is leaving Afghanistan?"

"Well, it's going to be a lot tougher for the CIA with them gone.

Tom replied, "I'm sorry to hear that."

Steve said, "It may mean we are going to be completely kicked out of Afghanistan after the army leaves. I won't be surprised at all, if that's what happens.

"Anyway, your vehicle we be there tomorrow afternoon."

"Thanks again, Steve, and take care of yourself and your people. I appreciate all that you have done to help us.

So now everything was in motion, the helicopters and their pilots should be here sometime this afternoon and the Land Rover would be here tomorrow afternoon.

Tom thought he should talk to Omar and tell him what Steve Troxler had to say about the possibility that maybe what al-Garde was really after was to take over Omar's castle, his land and his people.

That would certainly be a different reason for al- Garde to attack the castle than simply wanting to kill Tom and Jenny.

Omar and Grace were on their way back to Omar's office at the same time that Tom was headed there and they arrived at the same time.

Tom said, "Omar and Grace, I need to tell you something about my conversation with Steve Troxler."

Omar replied, "OK, let's go into my office and have a seat and you can tell me all about it."

Tom quickly explained Steve's thoughts on why al- Garde would attack the castle.

Steve said, "He's a leader and he has a bunch of men that are now without homes and no territory, so al-Garde wants Omar's castle and territory for him and his men."

`Omar thought about that for a minute after hearing Steve's idea of why he would attack the castle.

Omar said, "I think Steve may be right; it would make more sense than trying to attack my castle to kill two foreigners, who might or might not be in the castle."

Tom said, "Maybe my plan won't work if Jenny and I aren't his prime reason for attacking the castle the last time.

"If that's the case you may have to be in the Land Rover with us before he would attack again. What do you think, Omar?"

"I think you'll need me with you to make sure your plan has a chance to work, so count me in."

Grace said, "You're not going to be a sitting duck without me being by your side. you understand that, don't you ,Omar?"

Omar looked at Grace, then said, "Yes, dear, you'll be by my side."

Tom said, "Omar, you are a quick learner."

Jack added, "He better be."

16

Tom and Jack left Omar's office and went back to Tom and Jenny's suite, where Jenny and Serene were waiting.

Jenny asked, "OK, have you two got everything set now for our show tomorrow?"

Tom replied, "We think so, the helicopters and their pilots will be here this afternoon, thanks to Jack contacting the commanding general in Afghanistan.

"If you want something done in the army it helps to have a Pentagon three-star general asking it to be done.

"Then I talked to Steve Troxler and the Land Rover will be here to tomorrow."

Jack said, "Jenny, there is just one change in the plan. It seems Steve Troxler told Tom that maybe the attack on the castle wasn't to get you two, but to kill Omar and take over his castle and territory. So that al-Garde would have some place for him and his people to live."

Jenny asked, "What do you think, Tom?"

"Well, it makes more sense, since al-Garde doesn't have the area that they lived in anymore, after they were chased out of there by the army."

Jenny said, "So what does that mean as far as your plan goes, Tom?"

"It means that we're going to have company, Omar and Grace are going to have to be in the Land Rover with us, in case Steve's right and the real target is Omar."

Jenny said, "I understand that Omar's going to be in the car with us, but why risk Grace?"

Tom smiled and replied, "You'll have to ask Grace."

About that time they could hear the whirling blades of the helicopters as they were landing on the heliports behind the castle.

Jack said, "We better go down and check out Omar's new helicopters and make arrangements for the crews."

Serene added, "Yes, let's go down to meet the crews and let me check over the helicopters. I need to see if I can fly them."

Tom said, "I'm sure there is not going to be that much difference in the army's version than what you had in the Coast Guard"

The four of them rushed down to meet the crews of the two helicopters.

When they arrived they saw that the two crews were just checking out their helicopters.

The two crews had a total of eight men, four for each helicopter.

Jack said, "Thank you for coming to help us with this mission.

"I'm General Jack Hayes from the Pentagon, and the other folks on this mission are: Colonel Tom Parker, who is a CIA agent and his wife, CIA agent, Jenny Parker, and then we have. Lt. Commander Serene Sessions, from the US Coast Guard, now she is also a CIA agent."

The captain in charge of the helicopter crews said, "I'm Captain Milt Martin and this is, Captain Roy Brown, we are the pilots for your mission.

Jack moved closer to the two men and shook hands with the two captains, then was followed by all of the rest of his associates, shaking hands with the two captains.

Captain Martin said, "You'll meet the rest of our crew members later, right now they are busy taking care of securing the helicopters for the night."

Serene was the last one to shake hands with the two captains and she asked them, "I believe you're flying, UH- 60 Black Hawk's aren't you?"

Captain Martin, "Yes, that's right, are you familiar with that model?"

Serene replied, "Not exactly, I was in the Coast Guard and we had MH-60 Seahawks.

"I was wondering if there was a lot of difference between the controls on the two models.

"Also, if it's all right with you two, how about we go by first names since we are going to be working together. I'm, Serene."

Captain Martin replied, "I think that's a great idea. I'm Milt and this fine-looking gentleman is Roy."

Roy smiled and said, "Actually, Milt is the goodlooking one, but I'm the better pilot."

Serene said, "I think we're going to enjoy working together, because I need to teach some Afghan men to fly these helicopters."

Milt said, "Do you speak their language?"

"No, but fortunately for me, these men speak English."

Roy said, "I would say you're very lucky, because I don't think it's an easy language to learn."

Milt added, "Well this is my fourth deployment in Afghanistan and I still can't speak a sentence in their language."

Roy said, "Some people are just slow learners."

Milt answered, "You've got that right. However, I know how to fly helicopters, so Serene if you would like to take a look at our chopper, I'd be glad to show you, so you can see how much difference there is between the Coast Guard's and the Army's versions.

"Great, if you have time right now, I'd be glad to take a look."

"Time I've got, but I guess when I leave Afghanistan in a few days. I won't know where I'm going or how long I'll be there."

So the three of them walked back to Milt's helicopter and climbed inside.

The rest of the welcoming committee returned to the castle

Serene asked, "Milt, how long have you been in the army?"

"Fifteen years and Roy's been in twelve years.

Serene asked, "Are you staying until you retire with twenty years of service?"

Milt replied, "I'm planning on it, otherwise, I'd have to get a real job."

Roy said, "Good heavens, we wouldn't want to get real jobs, they might expect us to work or something."

Serene said, "How many jobs do you think you could get that you could get up in the morning and not have any idea if you would have people shooting at you or where you might be off to someplace else, before the day was over?"

Milt replied, "None that I can think of, not even police officers wouldn't know where they would be at the end of their shift, they would still know they were going home."

Roy asked, "So, Serene, how long were you in the Coast Guard?"

"Twenty years, I probably would have stayed longer, but I picked up a man out of the ocean one night and he said I should go to work for the CIA, so when I retired, I did."

Milt asked, "So how long have you been with the CIA?"

"I'm still a newcomer, I've only been with the CIA for less than a month."

Roy said, "You mean to tell us you've been with the CIA for less than a month and you're already out on a mission?"

"Well, I'm here to learn and work with Tom Parker, he's actually a retired CIA agent and became an agent after he retired from the army. He's the man I pulled out of the ocean after his plane crashed."

Milt asked, "If he's a retired agent, how come he's on assignment in Afghanistan?"

"Well, what I understand is that the President, you know the one that lives in the White House, asked for him."

Roy said, "Well, he must be something special if the President asked for him to do a job after he was already retired."

"Milt said, "Did I understand that the lady with him is his wife and a CIA agent, you know the Chinese woman?"

"That's his wife and right now she is a CIA agent. I heard that Tom had been wounded and was in the Army Hospital in Kabul and she shot and killed a guy who was trying to kill her husband in the hospital."

Roy said, "Wow, that's some story."

Serene said, "What I found out later was, that Jenny is far from just being a CIA agent. She's a Hong Kong Billionaire and they live most of the time in a mansion in Beverly Hills and to top it all off, she's also a lawyer."

Milt said, "Maybe when I retire I better see if I can get a job with the CIA, to see if I could get a wife like that."

Serene and Roy laughed at Milt's statement and Milt said, "Laugh all you want, but I could certainly take a wife like Jenny, that's for sure."

Then Milt got serious and began going through the Black Hawk's instruments and controls with Serene.

They spent over a hour going over all the controls and features of the Black Hawk and when he finished he asked Serene if she thought it was much different than the Seahawk helicopter and she told him she didn't think so.

They decided that they would wait until the next day for her to actually take it for a test flight.

Serene met the other crewmen and took them into the castle and introduced them to Omar and Grace.

Then Colonel John Strong met the flight crew and took all of the men to rooms that had been made ready for them.

Serene told Milt she would come to his and Roy's room and take them to dinner this evening.

Just before seven that evening Serene came to Milt's and Roy's room and when she knocked on the door, Milt answered the door and was happy to see Serene and her smiling face standing outside his door.

Serene asked, "Are you and Roy ready for dinner?"

Milt replied, "Yes, we are."

Milt started out the door with Roy right behind him.

Serene asked, "I hope you two are ready for dinner, Omar's kitchen staff puts out a lot of great food."

Roy said, "That's what folks say about my wife's dinners."

Serene asked, "How about your wife Milt, do people say that about her dinners?"

"Well, it's pretty hard to say, since I've never had a wife, not even a live-in girlfriend."

Roy added, "Sometimes I wonder if Milt is ever going to find a wife. I've known him for about ten years and he's never even had a steady girlfriend."

Milt said, "It's simple, I've just never found the right woman."

Nothing else was said as they stopped at the rooms of the other crew members so Serene to guide them all to the dining hall.

Soon they arrived at the large dining hall and then all of them were seated and Omar's staff begin serving dinner and conversations came to a close.

17

A few minutes later the dining hall was filled and the kitchen staff begin bringing food to each of the tables.

Milt asked, "Serene, where is the warlord that I have heard about that owns this castle?"

"Well, Milt so far he hasn't made an appearance yet, and when he does, you will not be able to confuse him from the rest of the Afghans, he's at least six-foot, seven and towers above everyone else in the building.

"He also just married an America girl that will be by his side, she's about five-foot, two and beautiful."

Milt asked, "Is she as pretty as you are?"

Serene replied, "I guess you will have to make that decision for yourself. So you think I'm pretty?"

"You certainly are. I think you about the most beautiful girl. I've ever seen."

Serene blushed and said, "What do you think, Roy, is that what he tells all the women he meets?"

Roy replied, "Well, it's hard to say, but the truth is, I've never heard him say anything like that about any woman before."

Then Serene said, "Do you guys have a routine that you worked out to try to impress a girl?"

Roy said, "Trust me, I've never seen Milt act that interested in a woman in the three years we've been together."

Milt just sat there looking at the two of them and the longer the banter between Serene and Roy went on, the redder his face got.

Serene said, "Thank you, Milt, that was a very nice thing you said about me. But you'll have to make your own decision about who you think is prettier, me or Omar's new wife, Grace. But whatever you decide about that, it was still a very nice thing you said to me."

Milt's face stayed red, but he said, "Serene, I love the way you look and I think you are the best-looking woman I ever met."

"Milt, I think you're a charmer. I think you're pretty special and we just met."

About that time, Omar and Grace came into the dining hall and the whole place became quiet.

After they were seated, the sound in the dining hall went back to where it was before Omar and Grace came into the room.

Omar and Grace just smiled and began eating their dinner. Then, Tom, Jenny and Jack, joined Omar and Grace at their table.

Serene said, "Milt, you know what I mean now, you can't miss Omar and Grace, they are a handsome couple."

Milt replied, "Yes, they are, you can't miss knowing who Omar is and his bride is beautiful, but not as pretty as you are, of course."

Serene couldn't keep herself from saying, "From your lips to God's ears."

The silence at their table was broken with laughter from Roy, Milt and the rest of the other helicopter crew members.

After they all quit laughing Milt said, "Well, Omar's wife is beautiful, but not as beautiful as you are, Serene."

Serene's face turned red and she didn't have another smart remark this time to come back to Milt with.

She just smiled bigger and tried to think about eating her dinner.

After everyone at their table finished their dinner. Serene said, "I'd be happy to show everyone around the castle if you would like to see it.

Roy replied, "I don't know about anyone else, but I'm kind of tired and think I'll go back to our room and watch some television. I saw the castle gets all kind of stations in English and we sure don't have that on our base."

The rest of the crew indicated they had somethings that they had to do or wanted to, so it left only Milt going on the castle tour with Serene.

As soon as all of the men except Milt left to go back to their rooms, Serene said, "So how much did you have to pay all of them to skip the tour?"

Milt replied, "Serene, you have a suspicious mind."

"No, I just know a lot about men, growing up with five older brothers. I saw how they worked if one of them wanted to be alone with a girl."

Milt said, "So how much did you get paid to leave, then?

"It would depend on which brother it was, the older the brother the higher the price, from a quarter to a dollar."

"Well you must have made a lot of money."

"Sometimes, Milt, I made more money from the girls that wanted to get one of my brothers alone."

"Serene, you have no morals, what-so-ever, you shock even me."

Serene said, "A girl does what she has to do."

They were now outside the castle in the courtyard where the helicopters were parked for the night.

Milt said, "Yeah, sometime a man has to do what he has to do."

Then he put his arms around Serene and gave her a passionate kiss.

The kiss lasted several minutes before he let her go and he said, "Serene, I've wanted to do that from the first moment I saw you."

She replied, "I glad you did, I felt the same way about you, I never felt like that before."

Milt took her in his arms again and said, "I love you and I want you in my life forever."

Then he kissed her again and she kissed him back."

When the kiss was over, Milt asked, "How are we going to make this work out with the two of us? I'm in the Army and you're in the CIA?"

Serene answered, "I don't have any idea, but we'll just have to figure it out, that's all."

Milt said, "Right now. I don't even know where I'm going after I finish this assignment of helping you train the Afghans to fly the helicopters.

"You know the Americans are all pulling out of Afghanistan. No idea where we are going to be sent."

"Yes, I know we are pulling out of Afghanistan, but somehow, someway, we'll figure it out so we can be together as much as we can, because I love you, Milt."

Milt replied, "You're right, we'll find a way so we can be together as much as we can because I love you too."

Then the two of them held each other and kissed again.

After the kiss Serene said, "We better get to bed, it's going to be a tough day tomorrow.

Serene guided Milt back to his quarters and they had one more kiss before she left him to go to bed.

Neither one of them was going to have much sleep that night and they would really need the rest before tomorrow came.

18

Sleep was something that was short of that night anticipating the events of tomorrow.

Tom, Jenny, Jack, Omar and Grace were all worrying about the battle plan that Tom had come up with to draw al-Garde out of his hiding place. What if it didn't work, what would they do then?

Tom went in and out of sleep wondering that if his plan didn't work, what they could do then to draw al- Garde out of his hiding place.

Tom said to himself, "No, it's got to work."

Jenny asked, "What did you say, Tom?" "Nothing, you are supposed to be asleep my love." "So are you, so what are you thinking about, Tom?" "Just doubting if my plan will work, what if al-Garde isn't even anywhere near here?"

"Tom, please try to go back to sleep. It's still just two o'clock in the morning and you need some sleep if you're going to be at your best tomorrow."

Tom reached over and pulled Jenny closer to him, gave her a kiss and said, "I love you, so you try to quit thinking about tomorrow and I'll do the same."

Tom kissed Jenny once more and rolled back to his side of the bed and did get back to sleep.

Then morning came like a flash of bright lights and Tom shot straight up in bed and saw that Jenny was still sleeping.

He leaned over and kissed her sweet face and she said, "Tom, is it time to get up already?"

"Yes, my love, it is, we need to get up and get moving so we can finish this assignment and go home."

"OK, but when we get back home don't be waking me up this early, OK?"

"I promise, when we get home. I will not wake you up to get ready to kill anyone, OK?"

"That will be good."

With that said, Tom got up and went straight into the bathroom as Jenny turned over, sat up and put her feet on the floor.

Then she found her bathrobe at the bottom of the bed, then slid off the bed, took her robe off the bed and put it on

She looked around on the floor, found her house slippers and put her feet in them.

Jenny then went into the bathroom as Tom was getting out of the shower.

Tom said, "The shower felt wonderful. I think you will like it this morning.

"I like my shower every morning and I know there is always plenty of warm water in Omar's castle."

Tom said, "You know what? We should give his castle a name."

"So, what name did you have in mind?"

"I don't know, but it should have a name."

"All right, love, what name shall we give it, instead of just calling it Omar's castle?"

"I'll let you know when I can think of one."

"That sounds fair. I've got to get in the shower and wake up more than I am."

Tom finished getting ready for the day before Jenny was out of the shower. He had dried his hair, got his hair combed the way he wanted it to look, shaved, brushed and flossed his teeth and had taken his morning pills.

Then Tom got dressed, it was certainly easier getting dressed being able to use both arms and not having to have someone help him.

He now knew how tough it had to be for people who lost their arm to do so many things he had taken for granted all of his life. He couldn't even begin to think about people who either lost both arms or were born without them.

What a way to go through life. He realized again how lucky he was to have totally regained the use of his right arm and to have had Jenny with him when he couldn't use it.

Jenny was soon out of the shower and getting dressed and ready for the day.

They left their suite and went down for breakfast and found all of their people were there already there, finishing their breakfast.

There was no doubt not many people had gotten much sleep last night.

Tom could see his people had spent the night thinking and worrying about how things were going to play out for the day.

All of them spoke a quiet hello to them as they entered the dining hall. Other than that, no one in the room was talking at all.

Tom recognized the anxiety that all of his people were feeling this morning and said, "Well, it looks like a great day for taking care of our business today."

Jack quickly understood what Tom sensed the mood was in the dining hall and quickly replied, "Yeah, it certainly looks like a good day for getting rid a bunch of trash."

Omar added, "Yes, some of that trash has caused me to lose some wonderful men, so it's time to take care of it today."

With that, the mood quickly changed; people began talking and smiling and became much more relaxed and enjoying their breakfast.

Tom got exactly what he wanted with a little help from Jack and Omar. Going into a battle, he knew it wasn't good to have everyone so concerned about what was going to happen that they would forget what their jobs were.

Now he knew his people were ready.

Breakfast was soon over and now they were waiting for the special Land Rover to arrive. Tom was hoping it would be sooner rather than later now that his people were ready to go.

When breakfast was over almost everyone went back to their rooms. Soon after Tom and Jenny were back in their room, Tom's cell phone rang and it was Steve Troxler calling from Kabul.

Tom answered his phone and said, "Hello, Steve, do we have a problem with getting the Land Rover here?"

"No, Tom, my man left here very early this morning and he should be getting there about noon."

"Thank you Steve, I think we have everything set here, we're just waiting on the Land Rover."

"OK, Tom, I wanted to give you a heads up so you can get everything ready. Do hope it works."

"Just one change in the plan. After talking with you, we decided Omar and Grace should go in the Land Rover with us in case it's Omar they're after and not me."

"Sounds like a good idea. I just hope you can get that son-of-a-bitch. Please call me and let me know how everything worked out just as soon as you can."

"No worry, I'll call you as soon as we see how this all plays out."

"Thanks, Tom. Again, good luck to all of you."

Tom said to Jenny, "Steve just told me that our Land Rover should be here about noon. So, we need to let everyone know that right after lunch we should be a go for our mission."

"Good, I'm sure everyone is anxious to get this over with so they can get back to their normal jobs."

"Well, there's a lot riding on this plan, so we're going to need a lot of good luck and a lot of prayers to be sure all of our people make it through all right."

Jenny replied, "Well, I think I've already said enough prayers for all of us."

Tom said, "I'm not sure we could ever say too many prayers to look after all of our people in this kind of task."

"I'm sure you're right, with so many people involved."

"Jenny, I often wonder what God thinks, while we are saying prayers to keep us safe, and intending to kill our enemies."

Jenny replied, "I know I've read in the Bible about all of the times He helped the Israelis kill their enemies, so I can only hope He feels the same way about us, and that He helps us do the same."

Tom added, "I hate to think of all the times in my life that I've had to ask Him to protect me. I'm sure He's probably thinking, how I get into so many places that He needs to protect me and my people, especially you, my love, but He's never failed me yet. I've gotten injured too many times, but I'm still here. Thank God."

Jenny said, "I do every day and I want you here with me all of my life. I love you so much."

Tom answered, "I love you, Jenny, let's finish this job and go home."

19

Ten minutes before twelve noon, the Land Rover arrived with the driver and the guard who both were happy to be arriving at the castle.

Carl, the driver, and Billy, the guard, were very happy that they had made it safely, and as soon as they had.

When they drove onto the castle grounds, and parked behind the castle, they were very happy to get out of the vehicle and be met by Afghans who spoke English.

They also saw the two US Army helicopters parked in the same area.

The Land Rover was checked over by two of Omar's men to be sure they hadn't picked up some of al-Garde's men.

It was clean and by that time. Tom was coming out of the castle to talk with the CIA men.

Tom recognized Carl as he had been the driver that brought him and Jenny to Omar's castle.

Tom said, "Carl, I see you drew the short straw again and were sent back here to pick Jenny and me up to take us back to Kabul."

Carl replied, "Actually, Colonel, I want you to know I volunteered to take you and Mrs. Parker back to Kabul. I think it's an honor to be of service to you, after all I've heard about your service to our country."

"Whoa, Carl, I think you've got the wrong guy, the one that's done so much for our country. I just do what they tell me, that's all."

"That's not what the CIA and the US Army says."

"Well, I guess. I'm going to have to quit paying those writers so much, they're making the stories too big and too good."

"OK, colonel, if you want it that way. I guess you know what you've done."

Tom said, "Let's get you and Billy some lunch and then we will see how well my plan is going to work to get al-Garde and his men."

Tom led the two men to the dining hall, where the rest of the folks who were going on this mission were already having lunch.

Tom went to the table where Jenny, Jack Hayes, Omar and Grace were seated and were waiting for him.

Tom said when they arrived at the table, "Folks, this is our driver, Carl and our guard, Billy, for our little trip this afternoon."

Each of the people seated at the table said "Hello."

Tom then said, "Everyone at this table will be riding with you except General Jack Hayes.

"He will be in charge of keeping all of us in the Land Rover alive and well."

"I can tell you, this will be my first time being looked after by a three-star general.

"Normally, I had to rely on privates and sergeants to keep me on the right side of the flower bed.

"Now, we have my very good friend, General Jack Hayes, looking out for us. I can tell you he will be doing a very good job. "I've known him for a long time and he's the best.

"I don't know of any other person, other than my wife, Jenny, who would be better to look after me than Jack."

Jenny said, "OK, Tom, you've said enough. Please sit down and have some lunch and let's get this party started."

Tom sat down next to Jenny and said, "OK, gentlemen, you heard what the boss said."

Everyone at the table began laughing and Carl and Billy quickly found seats and were ready for lunch.

Lunch went quickly and it was now time for the main event.

Tom said loudly, "May God bless and protect each one of you and we'll get this job done, so we can all get back to our lives."

Jack took over command of Omar's men and divided them up into two units. One unit would be going behind each side of the jungle to prevent any of al-Garde's men from escaping from the helicopters.

If any of them did get away from the firing from the helicopters, these troops would see that they didn't escape.

Jack would be in one of the helicopters to be able to coordinate the movement of the ground forces to be sure none of al-Garde's men escaped the trap.

It was time for everyone to start getting into their positions for the trap.

Serene and Milt oversaw loading a large amount of ammo for the helicopter's machine guns into each chopper.

Roy was busy making a last-minute check on the fuel for their helicopters to be sure they had plenty of fuel.

Carl and Billy refueled the Land Rover and checked over everything they could on the vehicle before they began their trip through the jungle.

Jack went over the equipment that all of his troops would need for their walk through the jungle.

Each man in the two infantry units now were carrying extra ammo and medical supplies.

The radio equipment was checked over again to make sure Jack Hayes could communicate with the Land Rover and the commanders of the two infantry units as well as with the two helicopters.

Jack was pleased that everything appeared to be operating correctly; everyone had extra ammo; he had communications between him and the Land Rover; the infantry units and the helicopters.

With Omar's help, Jack also organized a small unit to stand by in case any of the units needed help during the operation.

Jack went over one more time with Carl about when he was to stop the Land Rover and the signal he would give when he stopped.

Timing would be very important to get the infantry units moving to get behind al-Garde's men; and the helicopters flying to arrive when al-Grade's men were attacking the Land Rover.

Jack knew they needed to get to the Land Rover in a hurry after al-Garde's men began attacking the Land Rover.

He also knew that the armament on the Land Rover would be able to protect the occupants only for a short time, so they had to be there with the helicopters quickly.

OK, everything was as ready as it would ever would be.

It was time to get this show on the road.

Tom replied, "I think we need to go almost halfway between your castle and the main road."

Omar said, "Then I think we are getting close to the middle of the jungle."

Carl replied, "I'm pretty sure we are about halfway right now."

Tom replied, "Then let's shut the car down right now."

Carl didn't have to be told twice. He shut the engine off and let the Land Rover roll to a stop.

After the car stopped rolling, Tom said "Carl, I think you need to quickly get out of the car and raise the hood. Then just as quick, close the hood and get back in the car."

Carl asked, "Colonel, do you think I would be safe doing that?"

Tom said, "If I didn't think it was safe I wouldn't ask you to do it. I want someone to see the car coming to a stop and think we really had a problem with the engine.

"If you don't think you can do it, I'll do it myself."

"No sir, I'll do it and I can guarantee it will be the quickest look any engine ever had."

"OK, Carl. Just raise the hood, peer at the engine for a second, slam the hood down in contempt and get back in the car."

"Yes, sir."

With that, Carl pulled the hood latch out and was out of the car in a flash. He reached the second hood latch, raised the hood, took one look at the engine, slammed the hood back down, kicked a tire and got back inside the car.

Tom laughed and said, "Academy Award performance, Carl."

Carl just smiled and said, "Was that quick enough for your colonel?"

Tom replied, "It was perfect."

Next, Tom radioed Jack and said, "OK, we are stopped dead in the middle of the jungle."

"Roger, we will be waiting to see if you can draw some customers."

So, now they had to sit there and wait to see if al- Garde's people would find them and attack.

Fifteen minutes passed with no sign of anyone yet.

Thirty minutes passed and the people in the car were getting anxious, waiting to see if anything was going to happen.

It was now coming up to almost an hour and still no one came, when suddenly the car was hit by a small rocket on the left front door.

The car shook, then a dozen or more men came swarming out of the jungle on both sides of the car and begin trying to break the car windows.

When the rocket hit the left door. Tom called Jack on the radio and said, "The bees are attacking."

Jack replied, "Roger we're on our way."

The attackers fired numerous bursts of shots at the windows but the windows held.

Omar heard the leader of the group tell his men to get some type of explosive to use on the doors.

Two men rushed away to get whatever type of explosives the leader told them to get.

Everyone in the car was now getting concerned that the helicopters were not going to get there soon enough.

As the two men came rushing back with the explosives, suddenly out of the clear blue sky two helicopters came down spewing bullets from their machine guns.

A helicopter came down on each side of the Land Rover, and men were scrambling trying to get away from the barrage of bullets but no one did.

Tom could see some other men hiding back in the thick jungle, but they were getting away from the road as quickly as they could.

Tom radioed Jack to alert the units on each side of the jungle to be ready for the men trying to get away from the helicopters.

Jack radioed the men on the outside of the jungle that they had customers coming their way.

Both of the men in charge replied, "Roger, we are spread out and ready for anyone coming our way."

Next, Jack had the men he had standing by at the castle use their vehicles and come out to where the Land Rover was parked and divide the men up to make sure the enemy didn't try to come back to the road trying to escape.

With that, it shouldn't allow anyone to get away.

The helicopters would continue to patrol both sides of the jungle to make sure they didn't let anyone escape.

All of these actions continued for several hours and they had killed a lot more men than they got with the helicopters.

However, the helicopters did help the men on the ground find the enemy.

Tom had the Land Rover take them all back to Omar's castle after he was sure that there wasn't any more danger from al-Garde's men.

When they safely made their way back to the castle, Tom told them, "You were all very brave to be sitting ducks for these men that wanted to kill us all. I want to thank each of you for doing your part to make this plan work.

Some five hours later, Jack and all of men returned to the castle and had a report for Tom on the outcome.

Jack said, "Tom, your plan worked just as you planned it and we killed two hundred and fifty-seven men, but al- Garde was not with them. Sorry, Tom."

Tom asked, "Jack, are you sure al-Garde wasn't with them?"

"I'm sorry, Tom, but we found one of his key men and he told us just before he died that al-Garde left them last night and had planned to be back with them tonight."

"I'll be damned, I never thought he would leave all his men. I wonder what was so important that he left them.

Jenny said, "OK, you wiped out all of his men and he's wanted by all the different groups of people here, so he's finished hurting the government and the USA so we can go home now."

Tom replied, "I'm sorry to agree with you, but you're right, we didn't get our man, but he's pretty well finished here. So we will be going home like you said, love.'

Tom called Captain Roger Dean and asked him to get his crew together and come back to Kabul to pick them up to go home.

21

Two days later Captain Dean and crew landed in Kabul ready to take Tom and Jenny home.

However Tom said, "We will have a few more guests for this flight. We will be dropping off Omar and Grace in Hong Kong and picking up Tommy. Plus, Jack Hayes will be flying back to LA with us.

When they loaded the Gulf Stream in Kabul, they had to have Omar sit on the couch in the back of the plane and get him an extra-long seat belt to be safely belted in.

This was actually going to be Omar's first airplane ride. He, like almost everyone else who was going on their first flight, was somewhat apprehensive and excited at the same time.

However, he was seated next to his wife, Grace, a veteran of many flights, so she said, "It's OK to a bit scared of taking your first flight, but I'm right here beside you. It will be just fine."

Omar had never been afraid of anything in his life, so how could he be now? He wanted to tell Grace he wasn't afraid, but he couldn't do it."

Grace just smiled and took his hand. The door closed and the left engine started, then a few seconds later Roger started the right engine.

Then the Gulfstream started taxiing to the runway. Captain Dean paused, then pulled his plane onto the runway and the plane began traveling rapidly down the runway. Suddenly the front end of the plane lifted off of the runway and began climbing into the sky.

Omar looked out the window and saw the plane was now higher than the building they were going by.

The plane kept climbing and then Omar saw he was higher than the clouds. He said quietly to Grace, "We're higher than the clouds, Grace."

"Yes, we will be flying higher than most of the clouds until we get close to Hong Kong, then we will start going down and finally we will be landing on the runway."

"Grace, I never knew how it felt to be flying in an airplane, it feels strange to be so high off of the ground, but I kind of like it."

"Omar, thousands of people fly all around the world every day."

"I wonder how many people felt like I did, going on their first airplane ride?"

"I'd guess almost all of us did, I certainly did."

Captain Dean spoke on the speaker, "Tom, I have a radio message for you that you need to call CIA headquarters in Hong Kong when we arrive."

Tom said, "Jenny, I wonder what the heck they want?"

Jenny replied, "Maybe they got al-Garde in Kabul. That would be great news, wouldn't it?"

"It would be wonderful. I hope you're right."

Now, Tom and Jack would be thinking about what in the world happened in Kabul, since they left there only an hour or so ago.

Time on the flight was going by slowly after getting the information about Tom needing to call CIA headquarters in Hong Kong when they arrived.

Tom and Jack both wished the CIA would have just waited until they arrived in Hong Kong to contact them, so they didn't have to worry about what they were going to hear.

No, instead they were playing out all kinds of scenarios in their minds about what may have happened with al- Garde after they left Kabul.

The hours went by slowly by and finally Captain Dean announced over the speaker, "We will be landing in Hong Kong in about fifteen minutes, so if you need to use the restrooms, please do so now."

Not one of them made any effort to get up to go into one of the restrooms.

A short time later Captain Dean announced, "We will be landing in a few minutes, please be sure your seat belts are securely fastened."

Omar heard the doors open for the wheels to come down and be locked in places for landing.

Hearing that, Grace said, "Omar, that noise is OK, the pilot is just lowering and locking the wheels for our landing."

Omar smiled and said, "I glad you know what's happening with the airplane. I think I like flying, it's all right. It's so fast."

Soon after that, the wheels touched on the runway and the plane begin to slow down.

Then Captain Dean taxied the plane to the area for private airplanes and when they arrived, people from Hong Kong Immigration's boarded the plane and checked out everyone s passport.

Before they left they had had to get a passport for Omar. He had never needed one before, because he had never left Afghanistan in his life.

Lucky for him the CIA in Kabul got one for him. They had a picture that had been taken of him for his wedding to use for his passport.

The Immigration people quickly cleared all the people on the plane. Jenny knew they would, since they certainly knew who she was.

They would be here for a few days, so they would have time to have her company's name painted on her new plane.

OK, they were now off the plane and Tom called the CIA office and got someone on the phone he didn't know.

Robert Baxter said, "Tom, we've just gotten some information from the Kabul office that they found out al- Garde got a forged US passport and flew to New York.

"They also told us that he was bragging to the man who made his passport that he was going to be living on a island in America unlike any island in the world.

"One last thing they found out was that he had millions of US Dollars. He had gotten the money somehow and was bragging about him getting it from the US Government."

Tom asked, "Did they know when he left Kabul?"

"Yes, two days ago. We also know he cleared immigration's in New York this morning."

"Robert, do they have any information about if he had any other flight reservations from New York?"

"As far as we know he didn't have any reservations flying out of New York."

"OK, Robert, thank you. We do thank you for the information you got for us on al-Garde.

"I'll have to say we're going to have a lot of luck to find him now."

Robert replied, "From what I have been told by a lot of people with the CIA, if anybody can find him it would be you."

"Thanks, I can only hope they're right, and that we can find him, somehow."

Tom hung up the phone and said to Jack, "Did you get all of that."

"I'm sorry to say I did."

Tom said, "We'll be staying in Hong Kong for at least three days, because I know Jenny will need to get caught up on what's going on with her empire.

"I think you probably need to get back to the Pentagon and your lovely wife and not be sitting around waiting for us to take you back to the States.

"I think you're right. I'll contact our headquarters in Seoul and see if they can send me a plane to take me back to Washington."

"Jack, I really appreciate you coming to help me get al-Garde. I'm just sorry he got away from our little trap.

"I would like to know if he knew what happened to his men."

Jack replied, "I don't know how he would find out anything, since none of his men lived to be able to tell anyone about what happened."

"I'm sure you're right, I can't think of any way he could have gotten the information before he left Kabul."

Jack said, "Well, when you find him, be sure to let him know what happened to his men before he goes to meet them."

"I'm surprised, Jack, that you would think I would still be trying to find him."

"I've known you too long to know that you're not going to let him get away."

"OK, Jack so you know me too well, and you're right. I'm not going to let him get away with our government's money.

"At least I have a couple of clues, he's got an American passport with his name of it.

"We know he landed in New York and he's going to some island, unlike any other island in the world."

Jack said, "I'm surprised he used his own name on the passport, that doesn't sound like a smart thing for him to do."

Tom said, "Well, he probably thought we wouldn't have a clue that he managed to get an American passport and that we would ever have thought he would be leaving his men."

Jack replied, "Well, I guess he was wrong on both of those things. We know he left his men and the CIA found the guy who made his passport."

Tom answered, "Yes, but he doesn't know either of those things. I just have to figure out what island is different than any other island in the world."

Jack replied, "Well if anyone can figure it out it would be you, my friend."

By that time, cars had come to take all of them to Jenny's apartment buildings.

Jenny had Omar and Grace taken to one of her buildings located a couple of buildings from where she had her own apartment.

Jenny told the driver he was to be available to take them sightseeing and to various restaurants during their stay.

Jenny handed an envelope filled with Hong Kong money to the driver to give to Omar.

She told Omar, "This is part of your wedding present and if and when you need more Hong Kong money, please just tell the driver and I will have additional funds brought to you.

Omar tried to tell her that he didn't need her to give him money, but Jenny told him, "Your honeymoon is our gift for all you have done for us."

Grace understood what Jenny was telling him and told Omar, "Just say 'Thank you because this is what Jenny and Tom want to do for us.

Finally Omar said, "Thank you, my dear friends, we appreciate your gift and we will never forget it."

Tom said, "Omar, thank you so much for all you did for us and I told Jenny we needed to give your castle a name. You know your castle really needed a name but we couldn't think of one but I just thought of one: your castle should be called 'Omar's Lair'."

Grace said, "I like it, so now on our castle will be named, 'Omar's Lair'. Thank you, Tom, I love it."

Omar said, "So, 'Omar's Lair.' I like it, thank you, Tom. May God bless you and keep you safe."

Tom, Jenny and Jack got into another limo and the driver took them to LuTowers where Jenny's apartment was.

Another limo took the flight crew to another apartment complex, located near the airport, where all of them had their own suites.

Jack called the commander in Korea and asked if he could send a plane to Hong Kong to take him to Washington.

The commander told him he would make arrangements to have him picked up tomorrow to fly him back to Washington. When his plane arrived they would call him on his phone.

Jenny called her folks to tell them that she was home and asked them to bring Tommy over to her apartment.

Jenny's dad told her they would bring Tommy over after they finished dinner and that she needed to stay for a few days before going back to California to go over several new projects her company was working on.

She promised she would.

22

Tom was now in his and Jenny's bedroom in Hong Kong, trying to think of an island that was unlike any other island in the world.

The more he thought about it, the more he wondered, what could make one island so unique that theirs was only one like it in the world?

Tom had been on a lot of islands all over the world; each island had a beach; they were all surrounded by water which is what made it an island, and most all of them had vegetation of some kind and trees and rocks.

Then like a lighting flash, he remembered hearing about of an island in the USA, that didn't allow any cars, trucks, motorcycles, no motorized vehicles at all. That would certainly make it unique.

What was the name of this island, Mac something, right? It even had a famous old hotel on it, what was its name? It must be a grand place to still be in operation after almost two hundred years.

Damn, that was its name, the Grand Hotel, and it was on an island called, he almost got it, Mac, something. I remember. It's Mackinac Island and it's on Lake Huron in Michigan.

That's where al-Garde was going, it had to be, so that's where I'm going and I'm going to find him.

Tom couldn't imagine how al-Garde knew about this island, but, somehow, he knew about it.

Tom called Jack and said, "I'm going with you tomorrow. I think I know where al-Garde is.

"He's on Mackinac Island in Michigan, that's the island that's unique. It doesn't allow any motorized vehicles, they only have horse-drawn vehicles."

"OK, Tom, but I have to get back to the Pentagon, but we can drop you off in Chicago on our way to Washington."

"OK, that will be good enough. I'll make it from there."

Tom got on the Internet and found he could fly directly from Chicago to Mackinac Island, so being dropped on in Chicago would work great for him.

Jenny came into the bedroom and said, "Did I hear you talking to Jack?"

"Yes, I called to tell him I wanted to go with him tomorrow on his flight. I know where al-Garde is and I'm going after him.

"So, what makes you think you know where he is?

"Al-Garde gave us a clue when he told the man who made his American passport that he was going to the most unique island in the world.

"I know where that island is, it's in Michigan. It's a small island called Mackinac Island and it unique in all the world, because it doesn't allow motorized vehicles of any kind."

"Well that ought to make it unique all right. So how are you going to get there by going with Jack?"

"He's going to drop me off in Chicago and I can fly directly from Chicago to Mackinac Island and I will be staying at the Grand Hotel.

"Don't you think you can wait for me to finish my busy here in Hong Kong, so we can go together?"

"I'm afraid al-Garde might not stay very long."

"I guess you might be right, so you better go ahead and see if you can find him. I don't think he's going to have a bunch of men helping him, so I'm not too worried about you not been able to take care of him by yourself."

"Thanks, love, for your vote of confidence, that I can take care of myself against someone like al-Garde.

"I will certainly be careful, but I'm sure if I can find him. I will be able to finish my job.

"Tom, I'll make sure that Tommy is in bed, then I'll be in bed with you."

"Good, love, I'll be waiting for you.

Jenny was soon in bed with Tom and Tom said, "After you finish your business here, would you come to Mackinac Island and stay with me in the Grand Hotel for a week or so."

"I'll be there as soon as I can. I love you, you know."

"Jenny, they say the island is a very romantic place as well as the Grand Hotel. So, I think we might enjoy being there together."

"Any place I'm with you,Tom, is always a romantic place."

With that said, Tom took Jenny in his arms, then they were very romantic.

23

J ack picked Tom up the following morning at seven and then drove directly to the airport.

The Air Force pilot had called Jack and told him they should arrive between eight and eight- thirty.

Jack was now dressed in his dress uniform with his metals, ribbons and his three gold stars.

As they were getting out of the limo that Jack hired to take them to the airport, Tom said, "You look pretty damn good for a three-star general."

Jack replied, "Thank you, colonel, I'm happy to have your opinion on my uniform.

"Not, a problem, general. I am sure the Air Force pilots will be very impressed."

"Yes, they should be, they don't fly around three-star generals every day you know."

"I'm sure you're right, you will probably be the only one they will ever see."

"OK, we better straighten up now, before they think we're a couple of jerks."

"Yes sir, we are a couple of jerks, but we'll straighten up right away, sir."

About that time, the US Air Force jet pulled up to the private plane terminal and the ranking pilot came down a ramp to meet Jack.

When he arrived inside the building. He saluted Jack and said, "General Hayes, I'm Captain Barnes and I'm here to take you to Washington, sir."

Jack returned his salute and said, "Thank you, captain. This gentleman is CIA Agent Tom Parker and we will be dropping him off in Chicago on our way to Washington.

"Tom is in pursuit of a terrorist that escaped from Afghanistan and we're going to help him catch him."

About that time, two Air Force enlisted men came in and asked the captain, "Sir, do these gentlemen have some luggage to load onto the plane?"

Jack responded to the question, "Yes, we do have a couple of bags, airmen."

Jack pointed to their bags sitting next to the couch they had been sitting on.

The airman replied, "Thank you, sir, we'll take them for you."

Then he picked up one bag and the other airman took the other bag and they took them aboard the plane.

The Captain asked, "Shall we get aboard, sir?"

Jack replied, "Thank you, Captain," as he and Tom began following along behind the captain to the plane.

They were soon on the plane and a few minutes later they were airborne. Their next stop would be in Guam to refuel their plane.

Then they would make a stop at an Air Force base in California and then one more stop in Chicago to drop Tom off, before they made it to Washington.

Jack found they had three separate crews aboard the plane, so that none of the pilots or co-pilots would have to work the whole flight, they would rotate the shifts through the three different crews.

They would be taking on food at each of the stops for all of the crew members, as well as food for Jack and Tom.

For once the weather was decent across the Pacific, which didn't happen too often, plus they had a tail wind so they were making excellent time on their trip.

It would soon be time for them to land in Chicago to drop Tom off so he could see if he could catch up with al-Garde.

They landed and dropped Tom off at the private plane terminal and he made his way over to the airline terminals.

It didn't take him long to find a Delta counter to book a flight to Mackinac Island. His flight would leave in about three hours. So he found a seat at the gate he was to be leaving from.

He then called Jenny to let her know he was in Chicago and that he would soon be on his flight to Mackinac Island.

He told her that when he got checked in at the Grand Hotel and had a room, he would be taking a shower and going straight to bed.

His flight to Mackinac Island left exactly on time. There weren't too many people on the plane and he was able to go to sleep before the plane left the runway.

Arriving at the airport on Mackinac Island, he was soon off of the plane, grabbed his bag and went outside the terminal, where he saw a horse and carriage from the Grand Hotel waiting for him.

The driver took his bag and told Tom to get on the carriage and take a seat as he put Tom's bag on the back of the carriage.

It took some time traveling before they reached the Grand Hotel. Tom could see it was a magnificent-looking structure and with the longest porch Tom had ever seen in his life.

They showed him where to check in and Tom waited his turn to be able to go up to one of the very busy counters.

Soon, it was his turn and when he arrived at the counter, he said, "I have reserved the Musser Suite for a week."

The hotel clerk asked him his name and Tom told him his name was Tom Parker as he handed the clerk his platinum American Express card.

The clerk replied, "Yes sir, I have your reservation and the Musser Suite is ready for you. Would you like one key card or two?"

Tom replied, "Two, please."

The clerk made Tom two key cards and handed them to Tom.

Then he asked, "Is there anything else I can do for you, sir?"

"No, not right now; my wife will be arriving in a couple of days and then we may need your help."

The clerk then said, "We hope you enjoy your stay at the Grand Hotel."

Tom asked, "Do you know what's happened to my bag?"

"I believe it will be in your suite by the time you get there."

Tom went to the fourth floor and soon found the Musser Suite, and when he opened the door he found his bag had already made it to his suite.

Tom soon had his clothes off and was in the shower. After taking a long shower, he dried off, made his way to the king-size bed, pulled the covers and sheets down and was in bed and soon asleep.

Some eight hours later, he awoke with a pressing hunger. He realized he hadn't eaten anything for almost twenty-four hours.

He quickly got out of bed, dressed, checked the time and realized he had to find some food. He knew that he couldn't go to the main dining room, because he didn't have a suit and tie to dress for dinner, which the Grand Hotel required for men after six p.m.

He checked to see where he could go for some food and discovered he could go to the Cupola Bar.

He made his way there as soon as he could, looked over the menu and ordered. They soon had his dinner ready and his glass of Riesling.

Tom ate his meal in a very short time and ordered decaf black coffee and a dessert.

He signed the bill for his meal and then began to think about how he was going to find al-Garde on this very small island.

Tom wondered how al-Grade ever found out any information on this island in the first place. Al-Garde had never been out of Afghanistan before in his entire life.

He questioned in his mind if al-Garde was staying at the Grand Hotel; if so, how was Tom going to complete his mission and kill him.

Maybe he could just have him arrested and tried for murder by the Army for killing those American soldiers. Probably not.

Tom took out his phone and called Ron Parson, Assistant Director of the CIA."

Ron answered the call after a couple of rings and said, "Tom Parker, where are you?"

"Well, I'm on Mackinac Island in Michigan looking for al-Garde."

"Tom, why do you think he's there?"

"Ron, he told the man who made the American passport for him hat he was moving to an island like no other island in the world and that's Mackinac Island."

"What makes you think he in the USA anyway?"

"We are pretty sure he is because General Jack Hayes checked with US Immigration and they confirmed al- Garde arrived in New York a few days ago."

"OK, Tom so what do you want me to do?"

"I want you to contact the FBI and send some agents to Mackinac Island to help me find him."

"All right, I'll contact the FBI and have you some FBI Agents there tomorrow, where are you staying, Tom."

"The Grand Hotel in the Musser Suite."

"Of course you are. Is your wife with you?"

"No, but she is on her way."

"Tom, I don't think you thanked me for making your wife a CIA agent, the one who saved your life."

"Yes, Ron, I remember that you made her become a CIA agent and she did indeed save my life. So, thank you, Ron."

"Think nothing of it. I'd do it again to be sure I didn't lose my best and luckiest CIA agent."

"Sure you would, to be sure you covered your rear end and the CIA's."

"Tom, you know I love you and wouldn't want anything to happen to you."

"Yes, I'm sure that's true, if you didn't have me who else would you have to send out for these impossible missions."

"No one, so be careful my friend. See you in headquarters one of these days, after you finish your mission."

"Goodbye, Ron."

24

Ten o'clock the next morning the telephone in Tom's suite rang and Tom picked up the phone and said, "Tom Parker."

"Tom, my name is Lyle Morton, with the FBI, and my partner, Betty Jean Robinson, is with me. We are here to help you and we are in the hotel lobby.

"Do want us to come up to your room, or do you want to come down to the lobby."

Tom replied, "Please come up to my suite. I on the fourth floor in the Musser Suite."

Lyle said, "Yes, sir, we will be up to your suite, in just a few minutes."

About ten minutes passed and Tom heard a knock on his door.

Tom quickly made his way to the door and opened it.

Lyle said, "Mr. Parker. I'm Lyle Morton and this young lady is my partner, Betty Jean Robinson."

Tom asked them to come in and he guided them to his sitting room and invited them to sit down around a small dining table.

Tom asked them if they would like to have some coffee or tea.

They both said, "Coffee would be great."

Tom took two cups from a nearby stand, where the coffee maker was, and poured them coffee.

He asked if they needed sweetener or cream, both told him "No, thank you."

Tom said, "Good, I like people who drink their coffee straight."

Lyle asked, "Mr. Parker, I'm not sure that we know exactly what we can do to help you, but I was told you would fill us in when we got here."

Tom replied, "For a start, let's get to first names, mine's, Tom and you are Lyle and Betty Jean, is that right?"

Lyle answered, "Sounds good to me, is it OK with you, Betty Jean?"

"It's certainly OK with me. I'm either Betty or Betty Jean but my family has always called me, Betty Jean."

Tom said, "OK. That's settled, so here's what we are up against.

"There is a man by the name of al-Garde, from Afghanistan that was responsible for causing the death of several army soldiers some months ago.

"He has a forged American passport and passed through immigration in New York a few days ago.

"So we know for sure that he is here in the United States and we had a clue of where he was planning to go, since, he told the man who forged his passport that he was going to an island unlike any other island in the world.

"I believe he meant here, Mackinac Island, due to its unique laws about no motorized vehicles.

"Al-Garde, is a pretty smart cookie. He got us to thinking he was on our side and he was given the opportunity to organize and lead a company of his countrymen to fight with our soldiers, but then he caused the death of several Americans, and tried to claim it was an accident.

"Then he tried to kill me, but only wounded me. Then he and his people tried several more times, and then he escaped and fled to America.

Betty Jean asked, "So, how can we help you?"

"I need the FBI to help me find him, because you can ask questions as FBI agents that I can't as a CIA agent here in America."

Lyle asked, "OK, where do we start asking questions?"

"First, we need to find out if he really came here, and if he did, where is he?"

Betty Jean said, "Well, we could start by asking the ferry boat lines if anyone by that name boarded one of their boats."

Lyle added, "Also, I guess we would need to contact all of the hotels and guest houses, to see if they had anyone staying there with that name."

Tom said, "One problem with that is he may be using another name. However, I have pictures of al-Garde coming sometime today from the US Army, which could help us find him."

Lyle said, "Then we need to wait until we get those pictures before we start asking too many questions. Plus, we are going to need more FBI agents to help us.

"I'll contact our office in Detroit and request additional agents."

Tom said, "That's a good idea, Lyle. Another thing, al- Garde's English is not perfect, but it's pretty good.

"You will also need to check with the local airlines and charter flights, that have come here in the last week or so, to see if al-Garde was a passenger.

"I just had another thought, al-Garde maybe using a different name so the pictures will be critical in finding him.

"OK, just one more thing, he will probably be paying for everything in cash. I understand he's got a lot of the army's cash. I don't know how, but I was told he stole a lot of our money."

Betty Jean said, "That's a lot more information than we usually have when we are trying to locate a suspect."

Tom said, "You probably don't get involved very often with the CIA, but we usually know a lot about the people we're after, but some still get away from us for a while. However, we normally always get them, one way or another."

Lyle replied, "No, we've never been involved with the CIA until now, so I hope we can stay up with your standards."

"I'm sure you can, but working in the USA, is a little out of our jurisdiction, so we really need your help."

Betty Jean replied, "You can be sure we will be on our best behavior working with you."

Tom laughed and said, "I'm sure you will, since the President of the United States gave me this job of getting rid of said suspect."

Lyle replied, "We never heard a thing about any orders the President gave you."

Jean piped up and said, "Never heard about anything like that."

Tom replied, "No, I'm sure you never did or ever will.

"So until we get those pictures, I don't think you can do anything, but as soon as you have those pictures the first thing I think you should do is contact the ferry boats and the airlines and give them pictures and a number for them to call and alert you that al-Garde is arriving on the island or trying to leave it.

"Same story, second verse, contact all companies that offer flights off the island.

"But in the meantime, let's go down to the main dining room and have some lunch, by that time I should have the pictures from the army."

Lyle and Betty Jean said, "OK, let's have lunch and then we can get started finding your Mr. Al-Garde."

They had a wonderful lunch in the Main Dining Room in the Grand Hotel.

Betty Jean asked as they were finishing their lunch, "Have either one of you ever been in a restaurant or hotel that had a dining room as big as this one is?"

Tom answered, "No, I've never seen any dining area as large as this one and they still have some more rooms that are attached to the dining room they can open up. It's unbelievable how big this hotel is.

"Then there's the front porch. It's the largest porch in the world, at least I think it is."

Betty Jean said "This whole place is the most spectacular place I've ever seen in my life."

Tom replied, "Well, it's certainly the most magnificent and charming hotel I've ever stayed in, and I've lived in a lot of hotels all over the world.

"Then the horse-drawn carriages add another old- world feeling to the whole place. It's like being picked up in time and taken back to the nineteenth century.

"I kind of like it without the hustle and bustle of motor vehicles. However, they do have to have several people with shovels and brooms and two-wheel carts to pick up the horse droppings, but it certainly gives people jobs, that's for sure.

"Oh, yeah, and you can't forget the personal use vehicles. The bicycle, there are thousands of them; you can buy them, you can repair them, you can rent them, you can even get a bicycle built for two if you have a partner.

"If you not careful you can even get run over by them, they're everywhere."

They made their way back to Tom's room and he checked his iPad for any communications from the army and there were five different pictures of al-Garde.

Tom said, "Let's go down to the photo shop that I saw when I came over to the island, it was close to the ferry boat terminals."

They quickly went back to the lobby entrance and asked the man in charge of ground transportation if he could get them a taxi right away.

They soon learned "right away" wasn't like hailing a cab in New York City.

However, it didn't take too long after the man called for a taxi on his two-way radio that a horse-drawn taxi made its way to where they were waiting.

Then, the carriage driver had to drive past them and go a block or so away from where they were waiting for him. He had to get to the area they used to turn the carriages around, before they could climb onto the horse-drawn taxi.

Tom kept thinking to himself, yes, we are back in the nineteen century and there is nothing that hurries thing along. They were now living in a different time. So cool it. OK.

He also found out that cell phones and iPad didn't work all over the island either.

It took several minutes before they arrived at the photo shop that Tom had seen earlier.

Tom asked the driver to wait for them. Then he had a better idea. He asked the taxi driver how much he would charge by the day to be available, just for them.

The driver thought for a while and said, "I would need about three hundred dollars a day to just be available for you."

Tom replied, "OK, how about I give you four hundred dollars a day, would that be fair?"

"Yes, sir, that would be very fair."

Tom asked, "OK, what is your name?"

"My name is Bud White, sir."

"OK, Bud White, my name is Tom Parker. Do you have a cell phone so I can contact you when I need you?"

"Yes, sir."

Tom said as he handed Bud a card and a pen, "Would you please write down your cell phone number for me, so I can put it on my cell phone?"

Bud took the pen and his card and wrote down his name and telephone number and handed it back to Tom.

Tom quickly added Bud's telephone number to his phone list.

While this was going on, Lyle and Betty Jean went into the photo shop and asked to speak to the owner or manager of the photo shop.

The woman they asked said, "My name is Frances, I'm the owner and the manager of the shop, what can I do for you?"

Lyle said, "My name is Lyle Morton and this lady's name is Betty Jean Robinson and we are with the FBI."

As he said that he handed Frances a business card showing he was who he said he was.

Frances asked, "What can I do for you?"

Lyle handed her Tom's iPad and showed her the five pictures of al-Garde that the army had sent to Tom.

Then Lyle said, "We need to make copies of one or two of the best of these pictures to help us to be able to ID the man in these pictures. He's wanted for an international crime.

"I thought you could tell us which one or two of these pictures you thought would be the best to help people recognize this man.

"We want to be able to hand out pictures of this man to several businesses here, because we believe this man is on your island."

Frances studied the pictures very carefully and said, "I believe this picture will probably be the best one for people to be able to recognize this man."

Then she pointed her finger at one of the pictures.

Just at that time, Tom came into the photo shop and Frances said to him, "I'll be with you in a few minutes, sir."

Lyle said, "It's OK, Frances, he's with us."

Tom just smiled and said, "Right, we're all together."

Then Frances asked how many of the picture they wanted?"

Lyle replied, "I think we probably need about 500 copies to start with, do you agree, Betty Jean?"

Betty Jean replied, "That sounds like enough for us to get a good start."

Frances said, "OK, I'll get started making copies of the picture for you right now."

Tom said, "Would it be all right if you just run us off maybe fifty or so right away?"

Frances replied, "OK, I can have that many in about thirty minutes."

Tom said, "Good, we'll wait."

Frances took Tom's iPad back into her photo lab and transferred the five pictures to her equipment.

Then she started running copies of the one picture she chose as the best of the lot.

Fifteen minutes passed and she brought out about 50 copies of the photo and asked, "What do you think, will these pictures be OK for what you need?"

Tom, Lyle and Betty Jean all agreed that they were exactly what they needed.

Lyle said, "We'll take all of the ones you have ready and come back before you close tonight to get the rest of the photos."

Lyle handed Francis his FBI credit card and she ran the card for the payment for 500 pictures.

After Lyle signed the credit card form, he took his copy of the form for his expense report. They were off to begin handing out the pictures and information on how to contact them.

25

When they got outside of the shop, Tom said, "Lyle, why don't you take about half of the pictures and contact the people who work with the ferry boat lines here, and Betty Jean and I can take the other half and go out to the airport and contact all of the airlines and the charter companies?"

Lyle said, "Sounds good to me and then I will contact the FBI Office in Detroit and ask them to send us some more agents to help us canvass all of the hotels, motels, rental houses boarding houses and rental companies."

Tom gave Lyle and Betty Jean, Bud White's telephone number, as well as his, and explained that he had hired Bud full time to help them.

Lyle and Betty Jean thought that was a great idea, so Lyle left them to talk with the people with the ferry boat lines, as Tom and Betty Jean boarded the horse-drawn taxi for going to talk with people at the airport.

Arriving at the airport on horse-drawn carriage time, Betty Jean and Tom soon covered the airline's counters, the charter flights offices and the general aviation terminal, so now all of those locations had information and pictures of al-Garde.

None of them had any record that al-Garde arrived on any of their flights.

Then Tom and Betty Jean returned to the area where they had left Lyle and he soon found them.

Before leaving the area, Lyle went back into the photo shop and picked up the rest of the pictures that Frances made for them.

Then they made their way back to the Grand Hotel and Tom said to Bud White, "I don't think we will be leaving the hotel again today."

Tom paid him four hundred dollars and said, "Can you please come to the hotel at nine tomorrow morning and we'll get back at it again?"

Bud replied, "OK, boss I'll be waiting for you at nine tomorrow morning. When you get ready for me I'll be back in the turn-around area for the carriages, just give me a call."

"OK, Bud, we'll see you in the morning. Have a good night."

Then Tom said to Lyle and Betty Jean, "Before we do anything else, let's stop at the front desk and ask if they have a guest by the name of al-Garde."

They showed the information that Lyle had made about al-Garde being wanted by the FBI and gave them several pictures of him.

The two people on duty, looked at the information and picture of al-Garde and said, "No, they didn't have anyone registered in the hotel by that name and they didn't recognize the picture of anyone that they remembered seeing.

They did promise they would talk with the other people who worked at the desk and would have pictures and information given to all of the other departments in the hotel to see if anyone recognized him.

The three of them had dinner together in Tom's suite and not long after they finished dinner, Tom got a telephone call from Jenny. She told him she would be arriving on Mackinac Island around two o'clock tomorrow afternoon in their plane.

She told Tom she had just arrived home in Beverly Hills after finishing up the work she had to do in Hong Kong.

Tom told her he was certainly going to be happy to see her and would be waiting for her at the airport.

Jenny said, "Well, I'm certainly looking forward to seeing you. I wanted to tell you, that before I came home. I talked to Omar and Grace and they told me they had a wonderful time on their honeymoon in Hong Kong.

"Since they were ready to go home. I had our plane take them back to Kabul the day before I came home."

Tom said, "I'm really glad they had a good time on their honeymoon. I was sure they would in Hong Kong, with you making certain they got to see everything worth seeing and be able to do some shopping there.

"It's a magic city, if mainland China doesn't screw it all up for the people who built the city and the businesses they developed."

"Well Tom, that's something we will have to be talking about when we get home. I think I'm going to have to move my folks and my first husband's folks to Singapore.

"I would move them here, but they would never stand for it. Also, I'm going to have to move my company there too.

It's getting too hard to try to keep working in Hong Kong with the way mainland China is trying to control the local businesses."

Tom said, "I'm sorry to hear that. I can't imagine you giving up your condos, especially your apartment with the wonderful view of Hong Kong Harbour. I loved that view myself."

"Tom, my love, I'm sorry to say it, but sometimes life doesn't go the way we think it should.

"Operating in Hong Kong now is not what we used to have, the government is trying to take over too many things. So when we are through finding al-Garde, we're going to have to go to Hong Kong and have a fire sale and sell all of our holdings and move as many of my employees as I can to Singapore."

"OK, Jenny, I'll see you tomorrow. We have to find al-Garde in a hurry, so we can go back to Hong Kong and get your company, your family and your employees moved to Singapore."

"Good night my love, I'll see you tomorrow afternoon. Have a safe flight, speaking of that, are our pilots up to flying you here tomorrow. It sounds like they have been doing a lot of flying, if you just got home this afternoon."

"Well, I've talked with Roger and he said, he was going to ask a couple of his friends to fly me here. They all work together and their wives are going to take Julia and Crystal's place. Apparently they were pilots and flight attendants with the same airlines that Roger worked for.

"So it should be OK, and besides, I told them I would pay for them staying at the Grand Hotel, so they will be getting a little vacation and getting paid for help us out."

Tom said, "Good, I'm glad Roger thought of that. Get some sleep and I'll see you tomorrow."

26

Six-thirty the next morning Tom's room phone rang. He turned over in bed and answered the phone and said, "This is Tom Parker."

Tom heard a man say, Mr. Parker, my name is Bill Taylor. I work at the Grand Hotel's Front Desk and when I came to work this morning. I saw the picture and the information about a man you are looking for, by the name of al-Garde.

"I'm sure I recognized him from the picture you left and he is staying in the hotel, but he's registered as Mr. Al Gavis, he's in room 312.

"We got his name and address from his US passport and he paid for a couple of weeks' stay in cash. I'm pretty sure it's the same person."

Tom said, "Thank you so much for your information, Bill Taylor. Will you be working all day?"

"Yes sir, I have been off for a couple of days and just came back to work this morning."

Tom said, "Good, I will be down later and I would like to talk with you about the information you just gave me."

"OK, sir, I look forward to talking with you."

Tom's mind began racing in several directions at the same time. First, maybe Bill Taylor isn't right. It's too good to be true; how can we get him without having a major gun battle in the Grand Hotel? Slow down, Tom, he thought, first things, first.

Be sure the man is really al-Garde; next, find a way to get him, if it is indeed al-Garde, without causing too big a scene in the Grand Hotel that might get other people hurt or killed.

Tom was pretty sure the hotel management would prefer that, so whatever we do we have to be sure to protect all of the other guests in the hotel.

OK, Tom, really, first things first, like get up, get dressed and go down to talk with Bill Taylor. Then, contact Lyle and Betty Jean.

So, Tom got up, took a quick shower, dressed, and made his way down to the front desk.

As usual, there was a line of people waiting to check in or out. So he waited his turn and luck was with him, because although the hotel had four clerks on duty at this time, when it came his turn, he got Bill Taylor.

Tom quickly made his way up to the desk and asked, "Are you Bill Taylor?"

Bill replied, Yes sir, how can I help you?"

Tom replied, "I'm Tom Parker and you called me to give me some information about one of your guests."

Bill said, "Yes, sir. I called you about the man you FBI agents are looking for. I checked the information that Mr. Al Gavis give me as his ID, which the hotel requires, and he gave me his American passport, which I made a copy of it and I'll show it to you.

Bill handed Tom the copy of the passport.

Tom only had to have a glance at the picture on the passport to tell that it was, indeed, al-Garde.

Bill said, "Do you think that's the man you are looking for?"

"Yes it is, Bill, you did the USA a big favor, now we only have to arrest him."

Bill then said, "He told me when he checked in that the only home address he had was the one on his passport, in Bangkok, Thailand.

"He said he had lived out of the country for so long he didn't have a home here in the states anymore."

Tom asked, "You said he paid in cash for a two-week stay, so what day is he scheduled to check out?"

"Let's see, that will be tomorrow."

"Thank you, Bill, you have been a big help to me and the FBI."

Tom returned to his suite and was now sure that not only did al-Garde come to Mackinac Island, but he was right here in the Grand Hotel, in room 312.

Maybe what he should do, was step back and let Lyle and Betty Jean and some of the other FBI agents that were coming to the island, just capture al-Garde and be done with it.

Tom just wasn't sure they had ever been up against anyone like al-Garde, who would have killed his own mother to avoid being captured and taken prisoner.

No, the only sure way to be sure of getting al-Garde was for Tom to be part of taking him out.

Tom called Lyle's room and got him on the phone.

Tom said, "Lyle, I've got great news, one of the men who works at the front desk just told me that al-Garde is staying in the hotel and he is in room 312.

"I went down to the front desk and talked with him, his name is Bill Taylor. Bill showed me a copy of the man's passport and one look at the picture on the passport and I can tell you it's al-Garde.

"It's obvious, he got a second passport somewhere with the name of Al Gavis on it."

Lyle asked, "So what do we do now, do we try to take him with the three of us or should we wait for the other FBI agents that are on their way here, what do you think, Tom?"

"I think we should wait, so we can be sure to keep all of the hotel staff and the other guests safe. We don't know for sure what kind of weapons he may or may not have."

Lyle replied, "I think that's a very good idea, we certainly don't want to get a bunch of people hurt or killed trying to arrest him."

Tom said, "You better call Betty Jean and tell her to meet you down at the Main Dining Room for breakfast.

"I don't think I should sat with you two, in case al- Garde comes down at the same time and he recognizes me.

"I really doubt if he would, because as far as I know he only saw me once and I was in Army fatigues.

Lyle replied, "No, he probably wouldn't recognize you in the custom-made suites you wear."

Lyle called Betty Jean and asked her to meet him at the entrance to the Main Dining Room for breakfast.

Tom left his suite and made his way down to the Main Dining Room and asked to be seated by himself.

They showed him to a table next to a window and he ordered his decaf coffee.

Tom then made his way over to the long serving tables of food and filled a couple of plates with scrambled eggs; hash-brown potatoes; bacon; wheat toast, butter and strawberry jelly.

As he was sitting down, he saw Lyle and Betty Jean coming into the Main Dining Room and they were seated on the other side of the room, a long way from Tom's table.

As Tom was enjoying his coffee after finishing his meal, al-Garde was being seated about halfway between Tom's table and Lyle and Betty Jean's table.

Tom looked al-Garde over very well as he was being taken to his table to be seated for breakfast; there was no doubt it was al-Garde.

A waiter came over to serve al-Garde some coffee and arrived at the table just as al-Garde was getting up.

Al-Garde didn't see the waiter coming up behind him and as he stood up from his chair, he crashed into the waiter causing the waiter to drop the coffee pot and the very hot contents of the coffee pot spilled all over al-Garde's leg.

AL-Garde began screaming in pain as the hot coffee hit his leg, then controlled himself and quieted down as several staff members came to help him and began to apologize to him.

Tom jumped up from his table, rushed over to al- Garde and pushed the restaurant staff people aside cland said, "I'm very sorry, sir."

He took al-Garde by the arm and said, "I'll take you to our doctor and have him treat your leg and get your clothes cleaned and pressed."

Tom continued talking as loud as he could, "I'll be back to talk to you staff members as soon as I have our guest attended to; at the Grand Hotel we don't treat our guests like this."

Everyone in the Main Dining Room had their eyes on Tom as he was helping the poor guest to have his leg attended to, including Lyle and Betty Jean, and then they quickly realized what Tom had just done.

They both left their table and went quickly out of the Main Dining Room and overtook Tom and al-Garde as Tom kept leading al-Garde toward the front of the hotel and holding him by his left arm.

Then Tom pulled his left arm behind his back as Lyle said, "Mr. al-Garde you are under arrest for having an illegal passport and several other charges."

Betty Jean put the handcuffs on al-Garde's left wrist as Lyle pulled his right arm behind him, then she put the handcuffs on his right wrist.

Tom continued holding his arms behind him and then he turned al-Garde around, so he was now directly facing him. Tom said, "It's taken me a long time to catch up with you, but I did.

A few minutes later twenty more FBI agents arrived at the Grand Hotel. Tom said, "Lyle and Betty Jean. I think you have enough help to take this man in without any more problems."

Lyle replied, "Well, you certainly made it a lot easier having hot coffee spilled all over him."

Tom give him his best smile and replied, "I had nothing to do with it. God took it in His Hands to rid us of this trash."

When the FBI, searched al-Garde's room, they found almost fifty thousand US dollars and bank deposits for a million, five-hundred thousand dollars in a New York bank.

Tom made a trip back to the Main Dining Room and found the waiter that al-Garde caused him to drop the coffee pot on when he got up from the table.

Tom told him he was sorry for making such a scene when he grabbed the man, but the man was wanted by the FBI and you did us a big favor allowing us to capture him without anyone but him getting hurt.

Tom said, "There is a small reward for information allowing us to arrest him and I believe your actions certainly aided us in that. Then Tom handed the man a thousand dollars.

Tom said, "Excuse me, but I've got to get out to the airport, my wife will be coming in very soon."

Tom called Bud White on his phone to bring the carriage up, since he was ready to go to the airport to pick up his wife.

They arrived at the airport just as Jenny's plane was being pulled up to the private plane terminal.

Tom soon saw Jenny coming down the staircase and headed right to him. He grabbed her and held her tight and gave her a big welcome kiss.

Then he said, "You're just in time for a great weekend before we go home. You have to see this place we're staying in for you to believe it.

"Oh, I got al-Garde this morning. The last time I saw him, he was leaving with twenty-two FBI agents.

Bud White got Jenny's luggage and then Jenny said, "We have four guests for the weekend."

So Bud helped the two pilots and their wives load their luggage in the back of the carriage and off they all went to the Grand Hotel.

After they had everyone settled in their rooms, Jenny and Tom made it to their suite. When they arrived, Tom's cell phone rang and he answered it and a woman on the phone said, "One moment please, for a call from the President of the United States.

Tom then heard, "Tom Parker, I wanted to personally thank you for capturing al-Garde. You've done another great job for me and your country.

In addition. I know you retired as a Colonel from the Army, However, as Commander-in-Chief of the Armed Forces, for your recent meritorious services to your country, I hereby promote you to the rank of Major General in the United States Army, effective this date, and further, issue you another Purple Heart for injuries incurred during your recent action.

"You're the kind of American that made this country great. Again, thank you for doing a wonderful job. God Bless You."

"Your new rank should give you a nice increase in your retirement. Congratulations, Tom, I mean, General Parker."

Tom could only say, "Thank you, sir. I'm glad I could be of service to you and our country."

That call ended and then Tom got a call from his best friend, Four-Star General Jack Hayes, "Congratulations, my friend, you did it again, great job.

"I knew you could do it. Now quit before you get yourself killed. I love you, you know, and you're the best.

"Oh, Tom, I got that fourth star, thanks to you. Say hi to Jenny for me and have a great weekend in Michigan.

"I also understand, the President just gave you a promotion to Major General, so congratulations, General Parker.

After Jack finished talking, Jenny said, "When we go home on Monday, we can only stay a few days, just long enough to say hi to my daughter and make sure everything is all right in Beverly Hills.

"Then we have to fly back to Hong Kong and move my folks and my late husband's parents to Singapore and sell all of my holdings in Hong Kong."

Tom said, "I hope we are going to get our son Tommy while we are doing all of this. I miss him."

"Well, I only left him with my folks, because I knew we were going to have to go right back to Hong Kong to take care of all of these things."

Tom said, "I understand that, he's a great traveler, but I'm sure he's happier to be getting all that attention from his grandparents.

"So, we are going to have a wonderful weekend in this beautiful Grand Hotel and enjoy what it was like to have lived back in the nineteen century?"

Tom's phone rang again and Tom answered it as he always did, "Tom Parker."

Tom heard the voice over the phone say, "Tom, this is your friend, Ron Parsons, you know with the CIA."

Tom said, "Don't tell me you've got another problem that you need my help on."

"Not right now. I just wanted to thank you for your help with our last little problem and to let you know, after we got Jenny's plane out of the Bering Sea, our people found someone installed a device to shut off the power to your engines, after it had been flown for some time. That's why your plane crashed.

"We got the two mechanics who were paid by al-Qaeda to install the device in Jenny's plane trying to kill you.

"They will be serving time for the rest of their lives.

"Also, tell Jenny, we noted her as a hero in her CIA file for saving the life of another CIA agent.

Ron continued and said, "I'm sure she'll be happy to know that and she can be sure if we need her services again, we'll be in contact with her. As you know, once you're with the CIA, you're in until you die.

"Good-bye, Tom, thanks again for doing your normal great job.

Ron hung up his phone as he said, "I'll call you when I need you."

Jenny asked, "Who was that on the phone?"

"You don't want to know!"

The End

www.ingramcontent.com/pod-product-compliance
Lightning Source LLC
Chambersburg PA
CBHW031603310726
48974CB00003B/791